## At Last He Found the Photo He Wanted.

She looked straight into the camera with velvety autumn-gold eyes. He ran a finger along the picture's surface, tracing the full curve of her lower lip. He'd kissed those lips, knew their shape and feel, could remember their taste. She had the power to stir him, even now when he knew she was out of his reach.

"Why you?" he asked softly, as if her image, so hauntingly displayed before him, might answer.

He held the picture up to the light. There was something there in those dark depths, some secret knowledge. Her look was vulnerable, almost wary. Of what? The heated taste of her desire was with him still. And that was dangerous. Dangerous for him . . . and for her.

---

**LAURA PARKER**

writes both historical and contemporary romances, and feels that writing, in whatever form, is as good or poor as the author's interest—the genre is secondary. She reports, "I began writing romances because of my enjoyment in reading them."

Dear Reader:

Romance readers have been enthusiastic about Silhouette Special Editions for years. And that's not by accident: Special Editions were the first of their kind and continue to feature realistic stories with heightened romantic tension.

The longer stories, sophisticated style, greater sensual detail and variety that made Special Editions popular are the same elements that will make you want to read book after book.

We hope that you enjoy this Special Edition today, and will enjoy many more.

The Editors at Silhouette Books

Published by Silhouette Books New York

America's Publisher of Contemporary Romance

# LAURA PARKER
# Dangerous Company

*Silhouette Special Edition*

Published by Silhouette Books New York

**America's Publisher of Contemporary Romance**

SILHOUETTE BOOKS, a Division of Simon & Schuster, Inc.
1230 Avenue of the Americas, New York, N.Y. 10020

Copyright © 1984 by Laura Parker
Cover artwork copyright © 1984 Howard Rogers

Distributed by Pocket Books

ISBN: 0-671-53703-2

First Silhouette Books printing November, 1984

10 9 8 7 6 5 4 3 2 1

Map by Ray Lundgren

America's Publisher of Contemporary Romance

Printed in the U.S.A.

# Dangerous Company

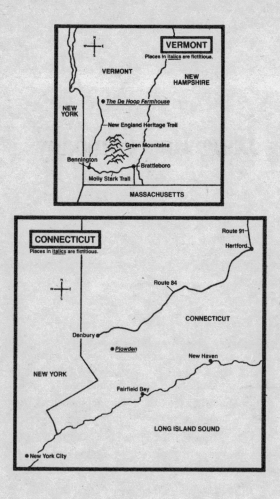

# Prologue

He didn't notice her at first. There were better tab-leaux for his artist's eye.

Pebbles rolled and skipped before the imprint of his wellworn hiking boots as he made his way down the steep rocky slope that led to the stretch of coastline. Soft, stone-washed denim rode his muscle-corded thighs as he strode easily from the reedy embankment down onto the fine gravel of the New England beach.

Finally he paused, took the long telephoto lens from the spacious pouch of his suede parka, and snapped it into place. He handled the expensive camera with the ease of a man long accustomed to thinking of it as an extension of himself.

Years of experience had taught him that people, like animals, were best photographed when they didn't real-ize his camera was focused upon them. The telephoto lens allowed him to experience the drama and immediacy of proximity with the added advantage of objective distance. It was the way he preferred to view the world.

Fall in Connecticut. He'd nearly forgotten the smells and textures of his boyhood home. The cry of gulls circling lazily overhead seemed sadder and keener than usual in the crisp air. On the horizon, the pearl gray waters of Long Island Sound were smudged against the paler gray of the sky. The scent of pine, of salt, of the frigid weather to come seeped into his consciousness as he recorded nature with the first roll of film.

He concentrated on the beach's human inhabitants with the second and third rolls. The click and soft *whirr* of the automatic forward of his camera had a rhythm which his mind's eye matched, framing the images he caught with each exposure. There was an elderly couple, bundled in sweaters and matching caps, strolling hand in hand well away from the water's edge. He caught the image of the laughter he couldn't hear, stole the look of years' long companionship that passed between them, and then recorded forever the configuration of their intertwined, aged hands.

She moved into his vision as he lifted the camera to his eye with a fresh roll of film. He never did "sugar shots." He had always left that for other, less talented, shutterbugs. He had been a photo journalist, with all the professionalism that title implied. Pictures worth words. That was his motto.

Yet he was arrested by the face that came into focus. She wasn't beautiful, at least he didn't think so at the time. Later he was to wonder at that.

She had been at the water's edge when he came down

the path. Now he noticed that she was alone. Hugging her sweater-clad body against the breeze, she was wading in the chilly surf that eddied in about her bare feet. Corduroy slacks rolled to just below her knees revealed shapely calves, slim ankles, and aristocratic arches. He smiled in remembrance of his father's saying that a high arch was a dead giveaway of a classy lady.

This classy lady was gritting her teeth in dogged determination. That was why he noticed the crescent-shaped scar on her left cheek. It was faint, a silver sliver upon the peach of her tan skin.

He smiled. The imperfection set her apart from every other lovely face he had seen.

As for her features, they registered as textural impressions: velvet-smooth skin, a soft fluff of golden brown hair held down by a white knit cap, a tender curve of cheek saved from coyness by the tense jut of chin. Her eyes, of indeterminable color, sloped down at the corners.

The sparkle of a tear did away with his final reservations about staring at her. The jutting chin trembled visibly and then stilled, as if some inner struggle had taken place and been won by sterner forces.

Adjusting the lens, he watched her jam her fists into the pockets of her trousers. Then she looked back toward the town, the way from which he had come, and his heart skipped a beat as she looked straight at him.

He couldn't put into words the feeling that swept him as she continued to stare, unaware that her gaze was locked with his through the miracle of mirror and lens. He'd faced armed rebels, looked down the barrel of more than one rifle during his years as a photo journalist, but never had he felt more vulnerable than at this moment. She seemed to see him, interloper that he was, trespassing on the private lives of those about him.

Her lips parted as if she would speak, perhaps hurl words of reproach at him, but he didn't care. For, in that instant, he felt a sudden hard throb of desire move down through him. Had she been within his reach he would have grabbed her, pulled her quick and hard against him, and caught that fascinating mouth in his own lips.

The uninhibited, unexpected surge of lust startled him into movement. He wanted to capture her image so that he might study it at his leisure. But the *click* did not happen, nor the *whirr*.

Stunned, he jerked the camera from his eye and realized with chagrin what had happened. Quite without conscious effort, he had already filled the roll with images of her. He looked up, a smile on his face, as if he could share the humor of his discovery with her, but she was no longer looking at him.

His gaze scanned the water's edge. When he recognized her, moving in the opposite direction, he was amazed by the diminutive size of her figure. He had thought of her as within an arm's—a kiss's—reach. In reality, she had been more than a hundred yards away. The tear had not been for him; nor had the inviting movement of her mouth that had stirred his latent desire.

He stared after her, his heels sinking into the sand, belatedly raising a hand to wave to her. But he didn't hail her. What could he say? *Don't leave, I want to know you*?

His arm fell limply to his side. He wasn't even certain

that was true. The only truth he could voice would be that he wanted her.

That realization gave him pause. It had been a long time . . . by his own choice. Even so, he was not a man who leaped to act out his baser needs. She'd probably call the police. He must be working too hard, he thought.

He smiled grimly, embarrassed by the last moments, and started back up the slope. His enthusiasm for observation was over for the day. Next time he'd confine his photo journalistic instincts to more innocent beach scenes and children.

# Chapter One

Mrs. Manchester? Yoo-hoo! Mrs. Manchester!"

Georgianna heard the call and hesitated on the top step leading to the house. A frown formed on her face. Though she had been Mrs. Edward Manchester for nearly a month, she still felt a sense of surprise every time she heard herself so addressed.

Turning, she saw Cora Walton, who had risen from a flower bed in the adjoining yard and was approaching. Her hair, cut Dutchboy fashion, was a pure shade of silver. As usual, her sturdy, compact form was dressed for gardening in smock and "dungarees," as she called her slacks.

"Mrs. Walton, how are you?" Georgianna called in her boyishly husky voice.

"Chipper. And I've told you to call me Cora." She tucked her hand spade into a pocket of her corduroy smock, then pulled off her garden gloves. "Let me help you," she said, and reached out to take one of the grocery bags Georgianna carried. "Called early this morning to remind you to be on the lookout for the fuel-oil man, but you'd gone. He came today."

"Oh, drat!" Georgianna replied. "I suppose I'll have to call him back."

"Not necessarily. The tank lines are curbside." Cora reached past the younger woman and detached a note from Georgianna's doorknob and smiled. "The man made his delivery. But you'd best check your reading to see that everything's proper."

Georgianna nodded. "Of course." She was house-sitting for a family named Rhoads during the next few months. No doubt the Rhoads had asked their neighbor to keep an eye on the sitter. It wouldn't do much for her image as an efficient, responsible person if she confessed complete ignorance about fuel-oil deliveries and such. "Thank you, Cora. Would you mind?"

"Certainly not," Cora responded, and reached for the ring of keys circling Georgianna's right pinky. "You could have had this delivered, you know. The Rhoadses are regular customers at Gresham's Grocery."

Georgianna chuckled. "If I didn't have little things like grocery shopping to keep me busy, I might take root in this house, never to be seen again until the spring thaw. The house practically keeps itself. In the weeks I've been here I've dusted just to keep limber."

"Poor dear, married so short a time and left alone," Cora responded sympathetically as she opened the door.

Scattered across the parquet floor of the entryway was the day's mail, which had been dropped through the door slot. Georgianna watched as her neighbor, a self-confessed sixty-two, nimbly bent and picked up the envelopes. It must be all that work in the garden that kept her so spry, she thought.

When Cora straightened up she glanced at Georgianna with a speculative twinkle in her eye. "Perhaps there's something here from your young man."

Georgianna shook her head as she started toward the kitchen at the rear of the house. "I doubt that. Edward isn't a very faithful letter writer. Besides, there aren't that many ports of call for his ship this time out. Come on back."

Cora followed her down the hall that led past the front stairwell and into the brick-walled kitchen of the expanded Cape Cod house. "Do you mean your young man doesn't flood his bride with letters and calls?"

Georgianna dumped her heavy bags on the tile counter with a sigh that had nothing to do with weariness. The disapproving tone in Cora Walton's voice had been echoed by others in the last few weeks. Each time she told someone that she was married only a month and that her husband was on maneuvers aboard a submarine in the South Atlantic, she received the same "poor dear" look. "It's not as though I've been abandoned," she murmured.

Forcing a smile, she turned to her guest. "Edward and I knew that we'd have only a short honeymoon before his months of sea duty came up. We'll have plenty of time to start life as a married couple when he returns. In the meantime, I'm perfectly delighted to have landed a job housing-sitting in this gorgeous place." She indicated the room with a sweep of her hand. "Edward is going to discover that I've developed an appetite for New England life."

Cora smiled a tight little smile that turned up only the corners of her narrow lips. "Edward's not a Connecticut lad, then?"

Georgianna reached for the bread dough she had left to rise beside the oven and began kneading it. *Mistake*. The subject of Edward always led her onto difficult ground. Didn't anybody mind his or her own business anymore?

"You're from Maryland, I believe you once said," Cora prompted.

Georgianna turned to Cora, whose no-nonsense gaze was gentled by sympathy. It was like facing a favorite aunt who'd just asked why you were dating a young man with a preference for fuchsia-tinted Mohawk hairdos and torn T-shirts.

*But she's not your auntie and you're not about to be drawn out.*

With as much cool politeness as she could muster, Georgianna said, "Did you have something else you wanted to tell me, Mrs. Walton?"

Cora's shrewd gaze narrowed, then she smiled, her face softening into matronly friendliness. "I guess that's telling me to mind my own business. No, don't apologize. I'm the worst busybody in town, and I know it. My Daniel, rest his soul, always said if our children hadn't moved so far away when they married, I'd have driven their spouses off before now. Just because we're neighbors until spring doesn't mean *you* must expect to live with me in your hip pocket."

Georgianna wiped her hands on a kitchen towel. "Oh, don't mind me, Cora. It's just that . . . I don't know quite how to explain it." *You certainly don't!* she thought.

Cora chuckled. "You need your young man to keep reminding you that you're properly wed. Unpacked a picture of him, have you?"

Georgianna was aware that any other normal young bride would have had the living room loaded with pictures of "her young man." Any other bride would have shown the entire neighborhood her wedding album by now. Another bride would not be stuffing her fists into her pockets to keep from betraying her annoyance at this perfectly normal curiosity.

"I've only the one. Upstairs," Georgianna answered as she studied the floor. "Would you like me to go and get it?" she questioned, with a pointed look at the bread dough sitting on the counter.

Cora understood exactly what her answer should be. "No, no, another time. I must be going. I'm expecting a truckload of fertilizer from the garden center. Oh, now I remember the other reason I called you. There's a country fair up near Windham tomorrow. I'm taking my babies up for the day. Thought you might like to come along."

"Would I!" Georgianna breathed. She was aware that Cora's phrase about her "babies" referred to her vast collection of African violets. "You're setting up a booth to sell violets?"

Cora nodded. "Just the standard varieties. No true violet collector buys plants by the roadside, but many of the local people buy flowers. Tomorrow, then? Eight o'clock sharp?''

A half hour later the bread was in the oven and Georgianna was in the basement peering doubtfully at the oil gauge on the huge iron tank. She was a person familiar with the technology of the second half of the twentieth century, including such things as gas and electric heat. The prospect of living an entire winter at the mercy of an antiquated fuel-oil furnace which provided steam heat was not comforting.

She ran a finger over the gauge window to clear away the grime and sighed in relief when she saw that the marker indicated "Full." The note attached to her front door said the fuel-oil man had filled the tank. Obviously, he had.

"I'm set," she murmured, yet her gaze drifted speculatively toward the bin of firewood in the opposite corner. The sight was not reassuring. There was only enough for two evening fires.

"After that, it's the axe, Georgie," she muttered, remembering the hefty stack of unsplit logs outside the back door.

Oh, well. That was what one expected, adventure and challenge, when one agreed to house-sit for the winter in Plowden, Connecticut.

The real estate agent who handled the arrangement had shown her the vegetable bins behind the root cellar door, which were brimming with carrots, potatoes, onions, and turnips. Behind another door was a wine cellar with dozens of rows of bottles laid on their sides. Still another revealed shelves and shelves of home canned goods—everything from pickles to jams to stewed fruit. The prospect of homemade jam to go with the bread she was baking lured her there now.

She ran her fingers over the labels that read ''Figs,'' ''Chutney,'' ''Spiced Pears,'' and finally grabbed a jar labeled ''Blueberry Jam.'' She had instructions to help herself to anything in the basement—but not in the wine cellar.

Upstairs in the butler's pantry was a rack with enough bottles of wine to keep her content for three years. Her absent hosts were nothing if not lavishly hospitable. But then, who else but the wealthy could afford to spend spring and summer in New England and fall and winter in sunny climes?

After depositing her blueberry jam on the kitchen counter, she grabbed the local newspaper, unread, and brought it into the living room with a bundle of logs.

A few minutes later, when she had coaxed a feather of flame from the white smoke of her expertly laid out fire, she sat back on her heels in satisfaction. Growing up in Maryland had not taught her about fuel-oil furnaces, but the Girl Scouts had given her a few lessons about survival. She meant to indulge in a fire every night until . . .

Georgianna rose to her feet. She was going to be alone for a while, and she had accepted that fact. There was no need to dwell on it.

There were certainly enough advantages in living here to make the loneliness less daunting, she decided as her gaze moved with admiration over the contents of the living room. The room boasted an imported marble mantelpiece, wainscoted walls, and parquet floors warmed by a scattering of genuine Turkish carpets. The furnishings themselves were a blend of antique reproductions and modern. The twin leather-wing chairs which flanked the fireplace were genuine antiques.

Every room in the house had its own theme, from the elegant dining room with its Chippendale pieces and Federal Blue walls, to the heirloom bedroom she occupied.

This was the kind of vacation any busy person dreamed of: months of seclusion to do whatever she wanted. Her list of projects was surprisingly long. All the books on her "must read someday" list were in a huge stack beside one of the chairs. Everything from Boccaccio's *Decameron* to Darwin's *Origin of the Species*, to Thackeray's *Vanity Fair*.

That was only the beginning. She had brought books to teach herself embroidery, origami, and cooking.

The aroma of baking bread drew Georgianna back to the kitchen, and with a smile of triumph she pulled the steamy nut-brown loaf from the oven.

*Not bad for a first try,* she thought as she thumped it and heard the hollow sound of doneness. Mastering the art of the yeast breads was also on her list of things to do.

When she'd set the loaf on the rack to cool and made a cup of tea, she went back to the living room and opened the cabinet door behind which was stored a built-in stereo. The flip of a switch dropped the waiting record onto the turntable and moments later the Baroque sounds of Vivaldi emerged from cunningly hidden speakers in the room's paneling.

"This is the life, Georgie," she murmured as she dropped gracefully down onto the bearskin rug before her fire.

It was a real polar bear bearskin, shot by some ancient member of the Rhoads family. It was a huge mass of white fur with claws and head still attached. The first time she saw it she had squealed, convinced that anything with that many bared teeth must have life in it. But, she decided, there was no reason to waste her conservationist's tears over a bear who had been dead longer than she'd been alive. As she stretched out to reach for a book she curled her stockinged feet into the soft fur with a purr of pleasure.

In another life she must have been a cat, she decided as she stretched out on her stomach and took a long sip of tea. She prized creature comforts to a shameful degree and now that there was nothing to stop her from pampering herself to her heart's content, she knew she'd become a slugabed in no time. Everything was perfect. She couldn't ask for anything more.

The phone sounded a discordant note that cut through the dulcet sounds of *The Four Seasons* and dragged Georgianna reluctantly to her feet. The Rhoads didn't believe in a phone in every room. The insistent ringing carried through the living room from the kitchen, where an old-fashioned wooden box phone hung by the pantry.

"Hello," Georgianna yawned into the long black mouthpiece as she stuck the funnel-shaped receiver to her ear.

"Mrs. Georgianna Manchester?" came the polite male inquiry. "This is Alan Byrd."

"Oh."

The disappointment in that syllable was not lost on the caller. "Were you expecting someone else, Mrs. Manchester?"

Georgianna shook her head, as if the caller could see her. "No, I just hoped." She brightened suddenly. "Has something happened?"

"Sorry, just the usual call. I've nothing to report. You promised to be patient, Mrs.—"

"My name's Georgianna," she cut in impatiently. "Call me by my first name, darn it!"

There was a short silence on the other end. Then, "I warned you that waiting would be the tough part. You convinced me that you preferred to do this on your own. If you've changed your mind . . ."

Once more Georgianna shook her head. "No, no. I'd just go crazy with company. I like the solitude. Do you have a date yet?"

"Sorry. Nothing's changed since our last conversation." Alan Byrd's tone changed from crisp efficiency to one of concern. "You're certain you wouldn't prefer to have company? Winters in Connecticut can be long and cold and dark."

"Send me a stand-in for Edward," Georgianna shot back. "Something in about a size forty."

"I don't think your neighbors would approve." His laughter was a little forced, but Georgianna didn't mind. At least he no longer sounded like he was talking to a child. "How about if I drop by this weekend?"

"Not on your life!" she answered. "You're right. I do have my reputation to think of, and Mrs. Walton is already watching me like a hawk. Lost a point this morning because I missed the fuel-oil man. By the way, what do you know about ancient furnaces?''

''Don't worry. They work on a thermostat, same as any system. Georgianna? You will call if you start going stir-crazy?''

''Sure, sure,'' she replied, ready for the conversation to end. ''By the way. You don't happen to have a wedding album lying around, do you?''

''What?''

Georgianna's laughter was free and easy. ''My neighbors want to see what sort of man leaves his bride five days after the wedding.''

Another long pause. *He certainly is cautious,* she thought in another surge of annoyance.

''Tell them you haven't received it from the photographers yet.''

''Brilliant,'' she murmured. ''Never mind. I'll think of something. If that's all . . .''

''I'll be in touch in a few days.''

''Make it good news,'' she replied. ''Good night. And thanks.''

The sound of the music drew her back into the living room—to turn off the stereo. The fire was no longer inviting, and she closed the glass doors. She didn't even glance at the book lying on the bear rug, nor did she pick up her half-full cup of tea. Her earlier contentment was destroyed.

She paused on the stairs as the sudden *swoosh* of the furnace's jets sounded deep in the bowels of the house. As the noise settled into a low ominous purr beneath her feet, Georgianna had the sudden image of a dragon sprawled in the basement. The old furnace seemed to be disgruntled, snoring uneasily as it spewed heat and smoke through the steam pipes which clanged and wheezed to life.

*High-strung and imaginative, that's what you are,* she scolded herself as she climbed the last few steps.

But she left the bathroom light on and the door half-open as she pulled the covers up to her chin. The last thing she saw before she closed her eyes was the gold-framed picture of a handsome young man. Blond and athletic in his naval officer's uniform, he looked like he was posing for a recruiting poster.

With a muffled curse word, Georgianna reached out and slammed the picture facedown on the nightstand.

*Chapter Two*

The mid-October morning was warm with sunshine as Georgianna stumbled about the kitchen after a sleepless night. The frosty chill of the past two weeks had given way to the season's last warmth; a true Indian-summer day.

Yet she scarcely noticed it as she buttered a slice of toast made from the fresh-baked bread. Those phone calls. How she hated them. It was impossible to relax with those not-so-subtle reminders of why she was in Plowden. She took a vicious bite of the bread, pretending that it was Alan Byrd's head.

When Cora rapped at the back door thirty minutes later, Georgianna had traded her robe for jeans, a mauve turtleneck, and a white down-filled vest embroidered with traditional ski designs. "Come on in. I'm ready," she said brightly, hoping that her carefully applied makeup hid the ravages of the night.

Cora's gaze rested a scant moment on her face before she stepped into the kitchen, but Georgianna knew what it meant. The dark color beneath her eyes might be hidden, but the dull luster of her gaze was another matter. Still, she was grateful when Cora's only words were, "You'd better bring a cap and gloves. The warmth has a way of disappearing with the sunshine, and we'll be home late."

Moments later, Georgianna entered the passenger side of a garish violet-blue van. She suspected Cora kept the monstrosity behind the closed doors of her garage in order to keep it from drawing a crowd. Not only was the metallic purple hue arresting, but there was a trail of deep green leaves painted along the lower edge. In black spidery script the name of a species of African violets was written on each leaf.

As they backed out of the drive, two young children jumped up from their play and began pointing and waving.

Cora smiled broadly and waved back. "Children love Billie Blue," she said as she patted her steering wheel. "I bought it right off the lot, you know."

"You didn't have it custom-designed?" Georgianna responded in amazement.

Cora's chuckle was surprisingly rich. "That's the trouble with young folk. You will never admit that anyone over sixty has a sense of humor. Of course, it was custom-designed. All those shelves in back aren't for storing groceries."

Georgianna glanced back at the racks that lined both walls of the rear van, now laden with flowering pots. Each shelf had its own fluorescent light and watering tray. "Why, you've a mini greenhouse on wheels!" she exclaimed.

Cora nodded. "I needed a vehicle in which I could carry my babies from show to show. Sometimes I'm gone for a weekend and it's not always convenient to store the plants indoors. When the heater in my old station wagon balked, I traded it for this."

She glanced from the street to Georgianna and winked. "*Saintpaulia*s aren't as fragile as rumor would have it. They're a hardy lot, natives of Tanzania, but they don't like cold. I told the salesman that I wouldn't pay for any extras, however. I needed solid dependability that would stand up to the wear and tear of soil, plants, and water."

"Is that when he suggested the lilac upholstery?" Georgianna questioned dryly.

Cora nodded approvingly. "Won't catch you sleeping a second time, hmm? As a matter of fact, it was the young man who'd brought his bakery van in for a tune-up who showed me the true possibilities. Now there was a van! It had racks as well as running water, a refrigerator, *and an oven!*"

"He didn't actually cook in the van?"

"No, dear. But he could keep a few bakery goods warm. Of course, it was his paint job that intrigued me. The van was painted to look like a giant loaf of piping-hot bread, complete with wisps of smoke curling up the sides."

"Very practical," Georgianna answered, smiling at

the thought of a giant loaf of bread having spawned a giant purple violet on wheels. "So you succumbed to the temptation, despite the cost."

"Not at all!" Faintly offended at the suggestion that she had succumbed to mere vanity, Cora said, "The young man explained that thieves are much less likely to steal a vehicle that calls attention to itself. A thief would find it difficult to cover his tracks while stealing a violet-blue van."

Georgianna wasn't certain the logic was flawless but she wasn't about to disagree at this point.

Cora smiled and patted the wheel again. "The painter was most uncooperative. It wasn't until I brought a plant to his shop that he finally understood the exact color I had in mind. Lost that baby—the fumes of paint and turpentine, you know. But in good service, good service.

"You think me an eccentric, and you're right. I've very little to occupy me these days with my Daniel, bless him, gone and the children married and away." Her glance was sharp and shrewd as she turned once more to the younger woman. "It's not good for any person to be alone too long. So, I've my babies."

Georgianna smiled politely and didn't answer. She doubted any plant could cure her discontent just now.

"What do your parents think of this young man who left his bride so soon?" Cora asked, switching subjects.

Georgianna shook her head with a wise smile. "My parents haven't met my husband. My father heads up his company's Pacific division in Indonesia. They've been in Jakarta for nearly two years."

"Didn't fly home for the wedding?"

"Couldn't," Georgianna corrected gently.

"And you couldn't wait, what with Edward setting out to sea. I see," Cora murmured quietly.

Georgianna inhaled deeply to keep her temper under tight control. She would simply have to get used to this. Cora lived next door. And really, aside from her intrusive questions about Edward, she was good company.

"I never asked exactly what I'm supposed to do today," she said after a moment.

"At a country fair? Surely you've been to one. Between local artisans and the antique dealers, I always come home with twice as much as I could wisely afford to spend. Besides, you look a little piqued. A day of sunshine and fresh air will be good for you."

The ride was a short one, less than an hour. Once Cora's table was set up, they put out rows of plants with velvet-soft leaves and blossoms ranging from violet-blue to wine to lavender to white. The violets were labeled with all sorts of improbable names, and Georgianna couldn't help laughing at one with moss-green leaves and double cerise blooms, that was named Wham Bang. Cora didn't entirely understand her amusement, and Georgianna had no intention of explaining that the name delighted her because it reminded her of a naughty joke.

"Now, go and have a good time," Cora directed as her first customers lined up. "But don't let your eyes grow bigger than your purse."

After only an hour of browsing the fairgrounds, which were owned by a local farmer named Wilburn, Georgianna could appreciate Cora's warning. In the vacant field, under the spreading limbs of gold and red maples, row upon row of long tables had been set up, and handicrafts of all sorts abounded.

She found an array of hand-sewn kitchen witches irresistible, as were the grapevine wreaths decorated with dried wild flowers and ribbons in shades of autumn gold, red, and brown. When she had picked out her favorite and it turned out to be more expensive than most, she reminded herself that the Rhoadses would not want anything less than the best. Every house in the Rhoadses neighborhood boasted a seasonal decoration on its door. She ignored the fact that she would take the wreath with her when she left.

Feeling quite virtuous, she passed the tables of home-made jams and jellies and pickles without a twinge of reluctance. The Rhoadses' laden pantry had nothing to do with it, she told herself.

The next unavoidable snare proved to be a table of sugar-maple candies. They had been molded into the shapes of maple leaves, grapes, and bears. One box for her, one box for her parents, and one box for her brother's children; the fourth box she bought simply to make an even number.

The smell of hot cider was welcome even though the heat of the pale fall sun had made her abandon her vest. The enticing aromas of apple and cinnamon combined pleasantly with the smell of burning wood and the acrid scent of autumn leaves. All in all, it was a perfect setting for the crowd that had gathered in Wilburn's pasture to buy and sell and generally enjoy the day.

It wasn't until she lifted her cup for a taste of the cider that Georgianna became aware she was being watched.

The pricking of awareness was too strong to resist. She turned her head to the left, as if summoned.

He was leaning on a forearm against the broad trunk of a tree, his body clothed in a cerulean-blue sweater and navy-cord slacks. There was a negligent grace about his stance, an attitude of indifference to his surroundings. Yet the moment their gazes met, Georgianna knew that it was he who had willed her action.

He was tall, with Mediterranean-dark skin and hair, and broad almost Celtic features that were at odds with his coloring. Georgianna's eyes widened in involuntary appreciation. It was an incredible face; angles of strength met broad planes of determination and were bisected by a jutting nose that looked as if it might have been broken. Ah, but the mouth. That full lower lip definitely spoke of sensuality. And his eyes were an odd color. Blue? Grey? Green? She couldn't tell, but she did recognize one thing. He was gorgeous! And, he was looking at her!

Later, when the stunning impact of the moment had worn off, she wondered what sort of picture they had made, staring across the distance of twenty feet as though they were alone. Now she simply submitted to the assault of his gaze.

His was no mere glance of appreciation. It sought recognition, formed a connecting link between them. As his hand clenched on the trunk of the tree, her palm tingled as though rough bark had gently scraped it.

Then his gaze altered. A faint smile curved the corners of his mouth, and Georgianna quivered with delicious sensation as her response sank down through her flesh. It was the most intimate glance a man could give a woman. It announced a knowledge of her that he couldn't possibly possess.

*Of course!* He wasn't looking at her. He was staring at someone he knew, probably someone standing right next to her!

Georgianna turned her head away. Released from the disturbing intensity of his gaze, she found herself flooded by chagrin. How embarrassing! She had stared at him, offering God knew what sort of invitation, when common sense should have warned her that he couldn't possibly have meant that disturbingly sensual glance for a stranger. She could only hope he was too interested in . . .

A quick furtive glance about gave her no clue as to the recipient of that . . . that *hungry* look. That was the only way she could think to describe his possessive stare. No man had ever looked at her in that fashion, as if he could devour her whole.

*Lord, what a fool you are, Georgianna! Practically drooling over a man who isn't even aware of your existence!*

Scolding herself in this vein, she moved rapidly away from the cider table toward the front of the Wilburn barn that served to house the items to be sold at auction.

The auction itself had begun more than an hour earlier, but she had viewed the stock and the only thing she thought she might possibly be able to afford was far down the list.

After finding a place among the crowd, she pulled the sales list from her pocket and ran her finger down it until she came to the number that the auctioneer had just called—number 125. She was interested in item 127, a Cape Cod rocker. A reproduction, of course, but once she sat in its deep saddle-seat and leaned against the high back, she knew she had to make an effort to obtain it. The one thing she had forgotten in her desire to spend a winter in New England was the possibility that her back might act up in the bone-deep cold.

Georgianna shrugged away the twinge that came to her now, as reminder that she had hauled a few logs too many up the cellar stairs the night before. It all seemed so far away now, the car crash that had badly injured her.

She had not quite believed it when an oncoming car veered out of its lane and headed straight toward her. She had reacted quickly, but nothing could save her. Severe back injuries had cost her her freshman year in college. Most of what she remembered of that year was months of hell as she struggled with pain and the desire to feel normal again. Finally that miraculous moment came when she was able to consign her back brace and cane to the attic forever. Now, other than an occasional nagging ache, which served as a reminder to be careful, and the single crescent-shaped scar on her cheek, she was whole again, and very grateful.

"Next item, number one twenty-seven on the sales list, a reproduction, circa 1900. A Cape Cod rocker, black lacquer finish, metal stenciling. Bidding will begin at twenty-five dollars!"

She wasn't surprised that a dozen people answered the auctioneer. Nor was she surprised that the bidding rose quickly to the hundred-dollar mark. She had promised herself to quit when the price reached one hundred and fifty dollars. At two hundred dollars she was wondering how many loaves of her own bread she would have to eat in place of regular meals. At two hundred and twenty, she began to have hope again. The voices had dwindled to three.

"Two hundred and twenty-one!" she cried gallantly, and was rewarded by laughter from the crowd.

"Bids in intervals of five dollars only, ma'am," the auctioneer reminded her.

"Two twenty-five," Georgianna answered with a shrug. She was planning to diet anyway.

For a moment there was blessed silence and her adrenaline flowed through her in anticipation of victory.

"Two thirty!"

The sound of that voice came as such a disappointment that Georgianna groaned aloud. Who? she wondered, swinging around to glare her disapproval.

He was smiling at her, this time with only six feet between them, and the knowing look in his eyes convinced her that he knew just how much his gaze affected her.

She turned away, her cheeks blazing. In that second she'd noticed many other things. For example, his eyes were blue, a vivid deep delft in his bronzed face. And, what was more, that very personal gaze *had* been meant for her!

She should be flattered. She *was* flattered, but she couldn't respond a second time. She was a respectably married woman. The ridiculous pounding in her ears that made her deaf until the auctioneer's third call for further bids was nothing but acute embarrassment.

"Two hundred and thirty-five!" she called out, unconsciously hunching her shoulders against the gaze she felt once more upon her.

"Two forty!"

The deep male voice, sounding so close to her ear, made her jump even before hands closed gently over her upper arms. To her further astonishment, he moved even closer, bringing his chest into contact with her back. "Allow me to buy it for you. I want very much to please you."

The good-humored whisper came as a warm breath against the sensitive spot below Georgianna's ear, eliciting a ripple of pleasure that spread across the surface of her skin. "See how easy it is to please me?" he prompted as his hands rose to enclose her shoulders.

Surprise turned to indignation as she realized that he was teasing her. He'd make a spectacle of them both if she let him.

"Two hundred and forty-five," she barked and then made an unsuccessful attempt to free herself by twisting her shoulders. The hands, warm and persuasively firm, remained.

"Two fifty and that's the final bid!"

There was a fleeting instant while she wondered why he was certain his was the final bid. Before she could believe it was happening, he spun her about by one elbow and into his arms.

At first she didn't react at all, inadvertently giving him time to curl one hand about the nape of her neck as his second flattened against the small of her back to pull her closer. She saw the laughter in his eyes as his face neared hers. And then it was too late.

The touch of his lips was a revelation. They weren't cool, as she expected, but warm, smooth, and dry. Their shape fitted her own softer, fuller lips to perfection. She scarcely heeded the rational thought that things had gotten out of hand. She knew it was an insane thing to do, to allow a stranger to kiss her, but she couldn't move a muscle in protest.

His lips moved to the corner of her mouth, his hands pulling her forward to stand between his feet so that they were touching from shoulder to knee. She heard him chuckle as the auctioneer called a second time for another bid.

She had instinctively shut her eyes at the beginning of the kiss, but they flew open now and met his laughing gaze. And then his lips were back, opening on hers, dragging them apart by gentle friction. The velvet tip of his tongue met hers as the auctioneer's third call went out.

Her heart pounding furiously, Georgianna lifted both hands, palms out, against the woolly fabric of his sweater, and shoved. Gasping for breath to give this presumptuous stranger a piece of her mind, she was reduced to mute consternation by the auctioneer's cry of, "Sold to the gentleman kissing the young lady!"

"You . . . you did that deliberately, to stop me from bidding!" she accused as realization dawned.

"The rocker's yours," he assured her calmly and, reaching out, lightly brushed her lower lip with his thumb, as if to remove the vestige of his kiss. "I promised to make you a present of it. You may claim it when I come to claim *you*."

Before she could answer he moved away, his arms

swinging freely in accompaniment to his long easy stride as he moved toward the auctioneer to pay for his purchase.

"Are you all right, Georgianna?"

She turned to find Cora watching her in concern. "No! Yes! Did you see that? Of all—all the unmitigated gall! And he—he—swaggers!" she sputtered, anger reducing her to stuttering.

"Aren't you acquainted?" Cora ventured with a speculative look at the man's retreating back.

"I never met him before in my life!" Georgianna maintained icily.

"Well, well. I admit to my surprise. The article did say he was in town to shake things up a bit. I wonder what his subscribers would think of such antics?"

Georgianna was unconsciously rubbing her mouth with the back of one slender hand. "I don't care who— What did you say?"

Cora smiled. "Come along, dear. People can be so rude. I'm certain they hope for more fireworks when that young man returns."

Georgianna had always believed that New Englanders were quiet, taciturn, and incurious. One glance at the gawking throng of bystanders was enough to convince her that either her belief was wrong or New England was being overrun by a more curious kind of American.

She walked ahead of Cora. The only thing that kept her from breaking into a sprint was the probability that her accoster might see her action and know it for the ignoble retreat it was.

"Can you believe that?" she huffed when she was inside the seclusion of the van. "I never met such an arrogant, high-handed boor. Suppose my husband had been here?''

Cora was squatting in the rear, reaching for the last of her plants. ''Maxim De Hoop never struck me as the kind who allowed convention to dictate his behavior. Yet, perhaps he didn't realize . . .''

''Not realize that there's a gold band—'' Georgianna raised her left hand to punctuate her words, only to stare in surprise at her bare ring finger. ''My ring! Oh, I must have left it in the soapdish in the bathroom.'' Perhaps Cora was right. Perhaps that masher had thought he was amusing himself with a single woman.

''That doesn't excuse him one iota!'' she said aloud.

''No, I agree. The day is glorious, isn't it?'' Cora suggested as she rose with two Baby Pinks in one hand and a Beau Prince in the other. ''The day, the merriment, and not all of the cider for sale is fresh, mind you. There's a kick to be had from the fermented sort.''

Georgianna thought about this for a moment, recalling the taste as well as the feel of that unexpected kiss. No. He hadn't tasted of fermented cider. ''He wasn't drunk. He's just a boor. And don't you defend him.''

Cora's silver brows rose to disappear under her bangs. ''Defend him? I hope not! I don't understand the new easy morality. Open marriages and living together. Bah! Oh, I know. I had my troubles with Dennis, my eldest. He and Rachel cohabited for nearly two years before they married. Cohabitation, indeed. Big words don't make it any more acceptable. 'Living in sin,' that's what my mother, bless her, called it.'' A serene smile curved her mouth. ''I like the sound of that, 'living in sin.' It makes it seem, well, more wicked.''

Georgianna grinned shamelessly. "You're a phony, Cora. And a softy. You actually thought that man was being charming in his own awful way."

Cora smiled beatifically. "Ever since he was a young boy, he's been a charmer. As well he should be, my dear. He has the background and breeding to be anything he wishes. That's what comes from being born into a dynasty."

Georgianna shook her head. "You've lost me. That man? Well-bred? Come on."

Cora glanced through the front window of the van at her table, which was nearby. "I've only got a second or I'll lose my customers. The young man who kissed you so thoroughly is named Maxim De Hoop." At Georgianna's blank stare she continued. "Didn't you read last night's paper?"

"Used it to start the kindling in the fireplace," Georgianna admitted.

"Oh. Mr. De Hoop owns that newspaper, as well as many other small papers along the Atlantic seaboard. His face was displayed prominently below the banner in yesterday's edition. He's in town to revamp the *Plowden Chronicle*'s format. I just hope he won't be tampering with my garden column."

Georgianna turned to gaze toward the auction barn. "You mean I was kissed by one of *the* De Hoops? They own that mansion at the far end of town, right?"

"Maxim's family home," Cora answered. "I never had Maxim in any of my classes, but I taught his younger brothers."

"You were a teacher?"

Cora nodded. "American and English history for

twenty-five years. Of course, the De Hoops have been a part of New England history for centuries.''

Georgianna thought about that dark face, those inordinately blue eyes with their knowing expression. ''He doesn't look Dutch.''

''There's a story to that,'' Cora agreed. ''Three hundred years ago the De Hoops were shipbuilders. The eldest son married the daughter of one of his Greek sea captains. On through the centuries the De Hoop men seem to have had a weakness for the exotic. I believe there was a Polynesian great-grandmother as well as another Greek bride.''

''That explains the unusual coloring and features,'' Georgianna murmured, deliberately driving that gorgeous male face from her mind's eye. ''I thought he looked, well, different.''

''A face no woman would easily forget,'' Cora agreed with just enough of a wistful tone to bring a blush into Georgianna's cheeks.

''Okay. So maybe I enjoyed it . . . just a little,'' she conceded. ''But from now on, I'll wear my wedding ring.''

''Aren't you coming back out?'' Cora asked when she had climbed down.

Georgianna shook her head. ''I've seen enough of the fair for today. Besides, I need to write a few letters.'' She held up her canvas bag. ''I brought pen and paper in case things slowed down. I'll be fine. Don't worry.''

''Give my regards to your Edward,'' Cora said over her shoulder. ''Tell him I think he's married a lovely young lady.''

Georgianna sat for some minutes chewing the plastic

end of her ballpoint pen. She had no intention of posting letters to Edward Manchester and she wasn't really certain what to tell her parents. After some thought she began sketching the fairgrounds instead.

She should have expected it, but it galled just the same. The sight of that lovely old rocker being tied to the rear rack of a white Lamborghini made her angry all over again.

*He would drive a car that's worth more than my entire life savings!*

She pressed her nose to the windshield for one last longing look at the rocker. It really was a shame that he had outbid her for it when he couldn't possibly need a reproduction of anything. No doubt, he had an attic full of originals.

Perhaps . . . if she explained to him how she was very flattered by his attention but, regretfully, was married, he might give her the rocker after all.

It was a moment of weakness that quickly passed.

*I wouldn't give him the satisfaction!*

He'd known just how to impress her without any hints on her part, she reflected sourly. If he knew how badly she wanted that rocker she'd never be rid of him. She had enough trouble just maintaining the Rhoads home and being creatively vague with Cora. The last thing she needed at the moment was an outrageously attractive man.

Georgianna's thoughts veered suddenly to a remembrance of the hard muscular contours beneath the woolly softness of his sweater. His eyes had been the exact color of that sweater. The wretched man had probably chosen it for that very reason.

Proud. Arrogant. Conceited. A number of disparaging labels came to mind, but none of them would stick. In her heart she knew that, had this been any other time in her life, she'd have thrown herself at him in giddy abandon. He had everything: looks, money, and *oh* what charm! But facts were facts. She was Mrs. Edward Manchester and she'd never thought much of married women who dallied. An innocent flirtation, that was what she'd experienced, and now it was over.

Georgianna sat back in her seat, ignoring the flash of chrome and white that streaked by Billie Blue a minute later. She was too busy doodling a name in the corner of her note pad. She'd written it with the scrolled flourishes it seemed to demand.

"Maxim De Hoop," she read aloud. *What a name!*

# Chapter Three

That's right, dear. Tap the side of the pot against the table. Not too hard. That's it. The soil's loose. Slide the plant out. There, find the spread and pull the clumps apart. Gently, gently. That's right. Perfect! Wasn't that simple?"

Georgianna nodded her reply. *Easy, my eye! How on earth did I get drafted into this?*

Of course, she knew. Cora had suggested that she could use an extra pair of hands in her greenhouse and old eager-to-please Georgianna had jumped in with an offer of aid. Little did she know she would be working with Cora's prize-winning plants.

"Put it here, dear. I'll brush fungicide on the breaks." Cora bent over first one and then another of the dozens of plants she and Georgianna had been separating, swabbing each. "I shouldn't have waited so long to separate these crowns. Now I won't have a full selection for the winter show. That will teach me to dabble in the yard while the real work goes begging."

"I never thought repotting could be such work." Georgianna slumped weakly against the opposite plant table.

"You're just too tentative. You're afraid you'll hurt them. You can't, you know."

Cora paused as a plant on the shelf above her head caught her eye. Reaching out, she viciously snapped off a brown-edged leaf and held it up to light. After pulling a three-inch magnifying glass from the chest pocket of her floral smock, she reexamined the leaf and her mouth became a pleated knot of disapproval. "I told the postman that last mail-order batch looked suspicious. Well, this lot must be dipped and isolated. I won't have mites!"

Georgianna knew better than to smile. Cora had a good sense of humor—but not where her plants were concerned.

"What can I do?"

Cora wasted no time answering that question. Georgianna spent the next hour potting the suckers and divided crowns in three-inch clay pots while Cora carefully measured and mixed an anti-mite solution and dipped the offending plants.

The sound of the front doorbell reached them via the electrical line stretching from the back porch to the greenhouse at the back of Cora's deep yard.

"Oh, bother!" Cora exclaimed at the second ring. She stripped off her gloves. "That must be a stranger. All my friends come to the back." She looked at

Georgianna and smiled. "I've worked you rather hard. We might as well pause for lunch."

Georgianna looked down at her watch. "It's two-thirty. I can't believe we've been at it for three hours."

The doorbell buzzed again. "Insistent, isn't he?"

"You're expecting someone?"

"No, dear, but men never give a person more than ten seconds between rings. He must have something very important on his mind. Coming?"

Georgianna nodded. "As soon as I finish this last one."

Five minutes later, when Cora had not returned, Georgianna entered the kitchen. She'd decided against sharing lunch. It was late and there was laundry waiting. She would just excuse herself and go home.

After pausing to rinse the soil from her hands, she pulled the scarf from her hair. A toss of her head made the waves swing out and then fall into place. It was her only vanity, her hair. It was as thick as a horse's mane and a rich natural golden brown that needed no help from coloring formulas. She wore it a little shorter than shoulder-length, liking the way it skimmed and swirled about her face as she moved.

The lower register of a baritone voice answered Cora's crisp New England accent as Georgianna passed from the kitchen into the entryway. Georgianna smiled. Cora had been right about the sex of her caller. And, to judge by the laughter that drifted out from the living room, she was extremely pleased with her guest. Georgianna would excuse herself and go home.

She stuck her head around the corner of the living

room entry. "Excuse me, Cora, I'll be going now. I finished . . ."

The man rose and turned very deliberately, but it took Georgianna only a fraction of a second to recognize him. He looked the same as he had at the fair, his dark hair windblown, his eyes so vivid a blue they seemed to radiate their own source of light.

This time there was no hesitancy in his response to her. His eyes moved down over her sweater and jeans, pausing at strategic places. "Well, hello."

For an instant Georgianna didn't move. The pleased note in his voice told her that the reason for his presence in Cora's home was anything but coincidence. He'd come looking for her!

"Yes, come in, dear," Cora seconded cheerfully. "I want you to meet Maxim De Hoop."

Involuntarily, Georgianna's gaze remained on him. He was treating her to the same hypnotic stare that had served him so well at the fair. The sight of his sensuous lips brought back a rush of memories. When they suddenly twitched in amusement, she flushed, realizing that he guessed why she was staring. "I–I'm finished, Cora. I'm going home."

The last was said in a rush, the words trailing out behind her as she drew back into the hall. A quick pirouette, and she was sprinting down the hall toward the kitchen even as Cora called her.

Damn! Damn! Damn! She hadn't thought she would ever see him again. Why on earth was he after her?

A trace of anxiety spread through her as she burst through Cora's back door and raced down the steps.

Why on earth would De Hoop have sought her out? After the fair, Cora had let her borrow the day-old newspaper to read about Maxim De Hoop. The article began with a mention of the newspaper empire which he had inherited upon his father's death a year earlier. It went on to explain that De Hoop had moved from paper to paper, working his way up the Atlantic seaboard during the past months in order to learn about his new responsibilities firsthand. What interest could a big shot like him have in her?

She began musing over the facts in her possession. As a publisher he had access to every news story that had come in over the press wires in the last few months. If he were a diligent man, he could know a great deal about her.

"Oh, Lord!" That look, that flash of recognition in his eyes, perhaps he had recognized her from a news article. Maybe he was hoping to gain her confidence and then pump an exclusive interview out of her.

Instantly, Georgianna rejected the idea of going in her own back door. He might be tempted to follow her if he thought she was alone. Instead, she cut across a neighboring yard and then swung around toward the street. It was early, not yet three o'clock. She would go for a walk in the park down the block until Mr. De Hoop had gone. Then she'd call Alan and tell him the worst had happened. She'd been recognized.

*What are you afraid of? He's just a man, after all.*

Georgianna wasn't sure she wanted to answer that question. She'd let him get the best of her three days earlier because she hadn't expected his aggressiveness nor the extent of his confidence in his ability to beguile. She'd never met a man who dared to treat a strange woman as he had her. What if she'd screamed, really created a scene, when he kissed her? What would he have done?

*But you didn't, you booby, and that's why you're afraid of him!*

He was dangerous, a danger to her safety as well as her peace of mind.

She'd walked the rest of the block and crossed the street into the park before she became aware of being followed. It was that same tantalizing sensation she'd had the first time he stared at her.

Ignoring the almost overwhelming urge to look over her shoulder, she jammed her fists in her jeans pockets and kept walking. She wasn't going to make anything easy for him this time. He could follow her to the ends of the earth, if he wanted to. She'd almost become the victim of a newshound because he had an attractive face, that was what galled her the most. She had been intrigued, momentarily, by a gorgeous male.

Her heel sank in a crack in the tar walkway and she stumbled, but the moment she regained her balance she began moving again.

This was ridiculous. He was still following, and obviously not about to give up until he talked to her.

Georgianna glanced about. Below her, beyond a stand of trees, a mother and her toddler were feeding bread to the ducks at the pond's edge. She was in a public place. The man couldn't be any more threatening than he had been at the fair. Besides, she knew who he was and Cora must know that he had followed her. There were witnesses, plenty of them, if she needed help.

Suddenly she paused and turned to face her pursuer.

He'd been trailing her by thirty feet and seemed in no hurry to close the gap. It gave her time to really look at him. He wore muted fall shades: a wintergreen and rust sweater, a cream-colored shirt which perfectly complemented the golden sheen of his skin. His slacks were russet corduroy. His clothes looked well-worn, as if he'd chosen them because they felt good rather than looked good. He didn't need to worry about coordinated dressing, she decided. He'd look good in a burlap bag . . . or nothing at all. Maybe better, in nothing at all.

That thought made Georgianna irrationally angry and the first words out of her mouth were deliberately insulting.

"If you followed me to apologize, then I'm listening."

He stopped a few steps from her, his smile deepening into a grin. "When you didn't return to Fairfield Bay, I thought I'd lost you. I've been waiting."

A faint unease touched Georgianna. *I've been waiting.* It sounded so inevitable, the way he phrased it. But why Fairfield Bay? She'd only been there once, the second day after her arrival in Plowden. She'd wanted to be alone to think about the enormity of what she had begun. How could he know about that . . . unless he had tracked her here from Maryland.

"I don't know what you're talking about, but I don't like people watching me." She folded her arms across her chest, deciding to play dumb about the real reason why he was after her. "You don't impress me as the Peeping Tom sort, but then I've never met one before."

Laugh lines appeared at the outer corners of his eyes. For a moment she thought he would say nothing at all. Then she noticed that his eyes had strayed to the swell of her breasts.

"I knew you would be the sort of woman who spoke her mind. A classy lady, that's what I thought the first time I saw you. Those long shapely legs, elegant little ankles with high-arched feet, yes, I said to myself, that's a classy lady. What I didn't suspect was that husky quality in your voice. That's quite . . . sexy."

"You don't know me well enough to say such things to me, Mr. . . . Mr. De Hoop." Georgianna returned coolly, hoping he hadn't noticed the deepening color in her cheeks.

He had. He moved a little closer and there was an inordinately pleased expression on his face. "I don't even know your name, but I mean to know that, and much more. I'd be a liar if I said kissing you once had satisfied my curiosity about you."

She backed up a step. "Are you so conceited that you think you can get away with harassing strangers just because you're good-looking?"

He looked around slowly, giving Georgianna time to realize that the mother and child had moved away from the pond's edge and that now no one else was within sight of them. When his gaze came back to her, it was bright with amusement and perhaps a touch of sympathy. "I'm not harassing you, you know. Doesn't that kiss give me at least the right to know your name?"

Georgianna held his look by sheer nerve. He was so damned certain of himself, and of her. Well, she wasn't unprepared this time. "The last time a man kissed me against my will was the night of college graduation. The guy was drunk. It was a sloppy mauling." Her voice was biting as she added, "Nothing's ever changed my opinion of unsolicited attention."

His eyes widened, the pupils expanding until they threatened to eclipse the bright blue irises.

He was not more than four inches taller than she, but the absolute confidence with which he moved made him seem overpowering. Reaching out, he ran the blunt tip of his index finger across her brow. The finger moved with mesmerizing languor from her temple to the ridge of her cheek, where he traced the faint scar. A ripple of pleasure went through Georgianna and her lips parted in surprise, despite her effort to remain unmoved.

*If this is standard operating procedure for his newspaper interviews,* she thought irrelevantly, *then he must be one of the best!*

He moved a step closer. "You were right. I came to apologize," he said softly, leaning toward her. "But I won't have you reminded of a drunken boy's antics when you think of me."

Three thoughts collided in Georgianna's mind: that he was about to kiss her; that she should turn and run away; and that she wanted very badly to erase his certainty that she could be seduced.

He took the decision out of her hands. His fingers curved under her chin, lifting her face. She half-stepped back from him but his free hand caught her by the waist, threading a thumb through the beltloop on her jeans.

"Give in, lady. It's only a kiss," he whispered a scant moment before his lips met hers.

Georgianna braced herself, thinking, *Okay, Mr. De Hoop, if you insist on this kiss, I will damn well make it memorable for you!*

At first he merely brushed the firm outline of his mouth over hers, as if comparing contours. "Lovely." The murmur eased out between his slightly parted lips and the warm fragrance of his breath filled Georgianna's senses.

His hand at her waist moved, the fingers fanning out over the top of her hip to urge her closer. He leaned his taller frame against hers, his thighs hard against the softer, feminine shape of her hips.

Against all logic, she welcomed the heat of his body. A sigh of contentment issued from Georgianna's throat. A moment of blissful pleasure ensued, until she remembered that her part of the lesson had not even begun.

The intimate contact was heightened when he insinuated his thumb between their joined mouths, pressing open her lower lip and exposing its inner softness to the stroke of his tongue. The jolt of fiery heat that resulted shocked her. She grasped him by the shoulders as much in defense as in aggression. The rich texture of dark hair tantalized her fingertips as she searched blindly for a hold, a way to stake her claim on him. The kiss went on and on, deepening until her lower lip was caught between his teeth. One hand settled at the back of his neck and, without quite willing it, her fingers began a gentle massage of the tense cords there. The circling motion seemed to relax him and his touch lightened.

She seized the moment. Twining her free hand in his

hair, she raised herself up on tiptoe. Her lips opened on his and she moaned softly. She felt his whole body respond, a response so explicit that it shocked her back into the reality of what was happening.

He hadn't expected her to jerk away and so she freed herself easily.

*Good grief! I must be mad!* she thought.

She was almost certain that he was a reporter after a story, or at least on the scent of one. In any case, she was not free to pursue a relationship with a man, no matter how attracted she was. Worse, she was behaving like a flirt, the kind who had no intention of assuaging the sexual fire she kindled.

Georgianna backed away from him, stepping off the narrow path into the grass, where her heels sank into the damp earth. But she hardly noticed. The man before her was rapidly regaining control of himself, much more quickly than she herself could.

Her fingers clenched into childish fists, thumbs tucked inside, and her left one touched the cool surface of gold. The reminder acted like a bracing blast of cold air. She did have a defense against him.

Georgianna met his gaze squarely. "If your apology is over," she said sarcastically, "it's time we introduced ourselves. My name is Georgianna Manchester." She raised her left hand very deliberately for his view. "Mrs. Edward Manchester."

She saw first surprise in his face and, for an instant, she would have sworn that the ring shocked him. Shame stained her cheeks. She was a married woman who had deliberately sought to arouse this man and now she was slapping him in the face with a fact he'd had no way of guessing.

She saw her thoughts reflected in his face as his expression changed rapidly from passion to surprise, to a momentary ugliness that made her take another backward step. The ugliness disappeared as quickly as it had come, to be replaced by a bland unreadable look.

"Married," he said quietly, and all of the dark, persuasive, sensual resonance of his voice was gone. "Well, Mrs. Manchester, I guess there's nothing else for us to say."

She couldn't quite believe it when he turned and walked away without another word. She had wanted that, hoped for it, but it still surprised and confused her. What was he thinking? Did he understand that she had never expected him to force the first, not to mention the second, kiss upon her? Did he hold himself responsible for what had happened? Would he leave her alone after this?

It was the last question that haunted her well after his retreating figure disappeared back down her street. Deciding to give him a good head start, she walked on down to the pond.

"Sorry, guys, no bread today," she told the flock of sleek, well-fed geese that came waddling toward her.

If De Hoop really were after a story, he would simply go home, lick his wounds while he thought of a new tack, and then return.

What if he wasn't acting as a reporter? What if, despite the unethical manner of his approach, he had simply been attracted to her?

Georgianna glanced down at the gold band she'd flashed so triumphantly in Maxim De Hoop's face. "This had better be worth it," she whispered.

"That's right! I said reporter, Alan! What're you going to do about it?" It had taken Georgianna three hours to get through to Alan and the wait had made her edgy.

"You have every right to be angry with me, Georgianna." Alan Byrd's voice was all sympathy again, which meant he thought she was getting overemotional. "I can't imagine what went wrong with the answering machine. But try to understand, you're not in any *immediate* danger."

"My call could have been a cry for help," Georgianna challenged. "You're only relieved that it wasn't an emergency. Don't try to talk me out of my anger. I wonder what kind of fly-by-night outfit you're with if you can't even get a damned tape machine to work!"

"This is no fly-by-night operation, Mrs. Manchester, but none of us is perfect. Now, repeat to me, slowly, everything you can remember about your contact with this De Hoop person."

Georgianna muttered under her breath. "I told you. A publisher named De Hoop seemed to recognize me at a country fair at Wilburn's Farm three days ago. Today he showed up at my neighbor's house. I happened to walk in and find him there. But I don't think for a moment that that was a coincidence. He followed me more than a block to the park, and then didn't stop until I confronted him."

"What happened then?" Alan prompted.

Georgianna thought about that before answering. "We talked."

"About what?"

"Things."

"Georgianna?"

"Oh, heck! He kissed me!" She blushed furiously during the ensuing silence. "Well? So what? It was against my will. I'm not exactly a candidate for a bag over the head."

"Georgianna? You called me about a masher?"

She gritted her teeth. "I . . . called . . . you . . . because . . . a newspaper man has been following me, for weeks. He said so. He said he'd been waiting for me to return to Fairfield Bay. I went there only once, three weeks ago, when I first came to Connecticut. He said he saw me there and has been looking for me ever since. Isn't that interesting? Or, is it acceptable behavior by your standards?"

"Don't get huffy."

"What if I'm being stalked by a maniac? I don't have any friends here, Mister Byrd. I could disappear for days before anyone would even wonder where I was. You're my lifeline. You're supposed to *do* something about things like this."

Another long pause. "Feel better?"

Georgianna paused. "I'm thinking four-letter words, Alan."

His laughter was the first reassuring thing about the phone call. "All right, Georgianna, I'll have your sex maniac checked out, thoroughly, by breakfast time. Shall I call at eight?"

"Seven."

"Georgianna?"

"Hmm?"

"Don't worry. If the guy's as well-informed as you seem to think, we can put a bug in the right ear. If he's innocent of everything but coveting his neighbor's wife, we'll have to leave him alone. It's safer. Okay?"

"Alan?" Georgianna said in her darkest, smokiest voice. The silence on the other end became electric. "Alan, go jump in a lake!"

# Chapter Four

*If* that will be all, sir?"

Maxim De Hoop raised his head and squinted at the elderly man in black. "I told you that would be all over an hour ago, Barnes. Why aren't you in bed?"

"I thought, perhaps, you'd require something in the way of a meal, after all." The older man's gaze quickly lit on his employer's nearly empty brandy snifter and then moved away. "Cognac always used to whet your father's appetite."

Maxim glanced at the perfect bubble of lead crystal in his hand and smiled. "It's left me with an appetite, all right. But there's nothing you can do about it." His smile broadened as he looked up at the older man. "My hunger is for something strictly female."

Phillip Barnes had been butler to the De Hoop

household since Maxim's father wore kneepants, and his greatest asset was his restraint in the face of the De Hoop temper. Beyond a brief moment of silence, nothing betrayed the momentary affront he felt at the crude remark. "I'll be retiring now, sir. Good night."

"Wait!" Maxim sat up. "Tell me something, Barnes. Why haven't you ever married?"

The older man's silver white brows rose. "But I did, sir. In 1929 I met and married Miss Althea Spencer. The Lord saw fit to give us twenty wonderful years before she passed away. That would be before your time, sir. It's a pity you couldn't have known my Althea."

Maxim saw tenderness in the man's thin face as he spoke his wife's name. It told him all he would ever need to know about their relationship. It had been a loving one. "I never knew. But, tell me. You've been a widower for more than thirty years. Why didn't you remarry?"

A rare smile tugged at Barnes's mouth. "For some men, one woman is enough."

Maxim turned away, his eyes focusing on the amber liquid swirling in his glass. *For some men there was only one right woman*. Depressing thought.

Barnes remained in the doorway of the living room a moment longer. He hadn't expected Maxim De Hoop to return to Plowden. After the funeral services for Maxim's father nearly a year earlier, the new heir had let it be known that he wouldn't accept total responsibility for the De Hoop family corporation.

That was Maxim. From birth, he was determined to have things his own way. Yet, here he was, delving even deeper into the family enterprise than anyone would have expected him to. Something very important must have changed his mind and, for that, the family was grateful.

A speculative gleam came into the older man's eyes as he gazed at his employer. Maxim was preoccupied, moody; nothing terribly out of character in that. But he was drinking more than usual, and he had never been known to turn down Mrs. Shepherd's New England boiled dinner. Barnes frowned. In his experience, nothing ever spoiled a De Hoop appetite unless it had to do with love.

Barnes turned away with a smile as that pleasant possibility lingered in his mind. It could be that Maxim's preoccupation had to do with a young lady.

When Barnes was gone, Maxim slumped down even farther in the elegant brocade Empire sofa. The stiff horsehair stuffing didn't give an inch.

"Damn museum piece!" he groused as he dug his elbows into the seat cushion and pulled himself back into a sitting position.

He glanced about the huge formal salon of his family home in disgust. Even as a child he'd been uncomfortable in this room. It was too tidy, too formal with its silk brocaded chairs and Waterford chandeliers. The acquisitions of centuries of sailing the globe were on display, from Ming vases and priceless Flemish tapestries to French commodes and Indian tea tables inlaid with ivory and semiprecious stones. The wall clock was genuine eighteenth-century Dutch.

"The damned room's a period set," he murmured. As a child, he and his brothers were only allowed in the room when they were summoned to play for company. In those days he had played the piano accompaniment to his brother Nik's violin. When Gustave, the youngest, took cello lessons they became a trio.

A grin of boyish devilment spread over Maxim's face as he drained his snifter for the third time that evening. Their final command performance had come during a Christmas holiday. He and his brothers had been away in boarding school, where the cello had been traded for an electric bass, the piano for an electronic keyboard, and the violin for drums. They may not have sounded as much like the Rolling Stones as they had hoped, but the comparison was more than enough for their mother. They were relegated permanently to the third floor.

The room and its contents had survived intact until now. "Maybe I'll sell the lot," he groused. He didn't have any need for the huge home or its vast collection. He had learned to live out of a suitcase years ago. But where to begin?

The first thing to catch a guest's eye was the formal portrait of Captain Willem Koenraad De Hoop which hung above the imported marble mantelpiece. Maxim's gaze moved there now. It was a solemn portrait. The broad high cheeks permanently reddened by the sea breeze were the only color in the fair face framed by blond hair and beard.

Maxim had always been fascinated by this particular ancestor. It was the eyes that caught and held his attention. That strikingly alive gaze, the exact color of his own, linked them by common blood and character.

The De Hoops were scrupulously honest about their ancestors, warts and all. Willem De Hoop had been a maverick, an adventurer, a man with the utter confidence of his own convictions. In a restless moment he'd suddenly plunged into publishing when two hundred years of family history tied the De Hoops to the sea. But he'd never looked back. He'd answered to no law but God's and his own. And, Maxim suspected, sometimes his own had come first.

"Things have changed, you old sea dog," Maxim said aloud as he moved toward the portrait. "There are no unconquered fields."

He shook his head suddenly. He must be more drunk than he suspected, talking to portraits. Yet he knew that great-grandfather Willem would have sympathized with him over the unattainable Mrs. Georgianna Manchester; the classy lady with trim ankles, a full, softly curved shape, a die-for-you voice . . . and a husband.

Maxim lowered himself into a nearby armchair. She was married. Why hadn't that thought occurred to him before?

He didn't often make mistakes and he didn't like the idea that he'd made so basic and simple a one as this. He'd always possessed a kind of sixth sense about women. Yet, nothing had clued him in, nothing at all. She'd led him on, he'd almost swear to it. And then she'd waved that ring under his nose.

He sat up suddenly. She hadn't worn a ring at Fairfield Bay. He could prove it.

It took only a few minutes to reach the carriage house at the rear of the main house. The summer after his freshman college year, he'd converted the old servants' rooms into bachelor's quarters.

When he turned on the light a dozen smiling faces, all female, gazed back at him from the walls. The pictures belonged to his younger brother Gus. Maxim glanced at the nearest one. Gus had never quite perfected the art of framing, but who cared? The girl, perhaps twenty, wore nothing but a big smile and a wet Harvard T-shirt.

As he moved across the room, he wondered fleetingly if Candace knew she was still captured for all eyes on a poster-sized blowup. No doubt she thought her wild antics of the past were locked away in memory. She and Gus were six years married, raising two children and half a dozen quarter horses on a few hundred acres of Kentucky bluegrass.

Maxim muttered under his breath. The word marriage was beginning to annoy him. When he reached the bedroom, he paused again.

An improbable bed carved in the shape of a schooner filled the room. A mattress lay where the ship's deck would be. The prow at the foot sported a figurehead of a coy mermaid. It was one of great-grandfather Willem's more eclectic acquisitions, one that had spent the greater part of the last century in the attic until the summer he had claimed it for his own.

Gazing at the mermaid's voluptuous form, he found his thoughts wandering. It took so little to stir his latent desire for Georgianna Manchester. She was incredibly female, so soft he wasn't certain he'd actually held her until their lips met. Then all he'd wanted was to get even closer.

That voice! Lord, it was like being touched by her. The gentle stroke of fingers upon his skin was in every inflection of that husky vibrato.

He drew in a hasty breath as desire, swift and strong, throbbed within him again.

His joy at finding her at the fair was only momentarily

abated when she disappeared. He knew how to track an elusive subject. He had seen his mystery woman vanish into Cora Walton's van and had known he could get Cora's address from the *Chronicle*. Without even waiting to plan his approach to Mrs. Walton, he'd gone straight there, knowing that she would lead him to Georgianna.

That surprised him. He knew he was acting like a fool, but he couldn't stop himself. Not when he carried the memory of Georgianna's reaction to their first kiss. He'd felt the slightest ripple of response when his hand touched her cheek just before he kissed her for the second time. In that instant, she'd been caught up as much as he by the passion erupting between them.

Years of snap judgment in desperate situations had created in him a sensitivity to the emotional climate of strangers. That deliberate act of waving her wedding band under his nose had been as much an act of defense against herself as against him. He'd read it in her eyes. That was what was tearing him apart now.

"I don't bed married women." It made him feel better to say the words aloud. Now that they were said, he remembered why he had come here.

In the darkroom adjoining the bedroom he flipped the switch and was again greeted by a dozen photos. This time they were all of the same woman. They were clamped up where he'd left them to dry.

His eyes ranged over them greedily, looking for a particular shot. When he found it, he grunted in satisfaction as he snatched it from the line.

She was brushing a strand of windblown hair back from her face. Her ring finger was bare.

Quite without reasoning why, he began mixing fresh developing solution. He'd only developed part of the thirty-six shot roll. Suddenly he wanted them all.

It was more than an hour before he had finished. At last, the final photograph was pinned up before him, still dripping with bath solution.

She looked straight at the camera, her eyes autumn-gold. He'd seen those eyes up close, where their startling depths were all the more visible. There was a slight frown on her brow, no more than a pucker on the ridge above her long straight nose. His eyes moved to her parted lips, and once more desire jolted him.

He ran a finger along the picture's surface, tracing the full curve of her lower lip. He'd kissed those lips, knew their shape and feel, could remember their taste. She had the power to stir him, even now when he knew she was out of bounds.

"Why you?" he asked softly, as if her image, so hauntingly displayed before him, might answer.

He'd wanted her before he ever heard her voice, ever knew the exact color of her eyes, ever touched her. Had he wanted something she represented? A challenge? Perhaps. A relief from the pressures of the job he had inherited? More likely.

Too many things were changing too quickly in his life. He felt suspended between his former life of high-speed adventure and independence, and his new responsibility as head of the De Hoop Corporation and family.

No wonder a fantasy had taken root. For all he knew, the lady of his imaginings did not exist.

The thought startled him. He snatched the picture and held it up to the light, as if he could read the mystery in her eyes. There was something there, in those dark depths, some secret knowledge that pricked his journalist's sixth sense. She looked so alone, as if waiting for something—or someone—yet to come. Behind that cool facade lurked uncommon passion, he'd bet on it. Yet her look was vulnerable, almost wary. Of what?

"Oh, God!" Maxim groaned in disgust with himself and dropped the picture. Speculation was ridiculous. And dangerous. It was ridiculous because he had no intention of ever going near her again. It was dangerous because just the wild suspicion that she might be unhappily married had set his pulse racing.

If she were not happy, the dark side of him reasoned, then she would be looking for happiness.

The heated taste of her lips was with him still. And that was dangerous. Dangerous for him . . . and for her.

# Chapter Five

"Satisfied?"

"I'm not certain," Georgianna mumbled. It was 7:09 A.M., much too early for Alan Byrd's I-told-you-so tone of voice to go over well. "Read me the first part again."

"Which part, where it says Maxim Constantine De Hoop is not married? Or that he's filthy rich? Or how about the part where that slick woman's magazine voted him one of ten Hunks of the Year? Or—"

"Oh, let's forget the whole thing!" she inserted sourly.

"Grumpy . . . in . . . the . . . morning." Alan's delivery hinted he was writing the words down.

"Don't you dare!" she cried in irritation. "My file with you people is already bursting with little tidbits. I'll bet you even know what sort of toothpaste I use." When Alan calmly gave the right answer, Georgianna exploded. "Good grief! Is nothing sacred, nothing too personal? Oh, I think I'm going to be sick!"

The receiver landed in its cradle with a bang. Immediately the phone began to ring. She eyed it for ten rings before she picked it up again. "I'm not sick!" she barked.

"I'm glad to hear it." There was a slight pause during which Georgianna realized that the male voice on the line this time was not Alan's.

"Who is this?" she demanded, annoyed and embarrassed that a stranger had been subjected to her anger.

"Maxim De Hoop." Another pause. "You didn't hang up." He sounded genuinely pleased.

"Should I have?" She sounded cold and distant, but there was nothing the least bit detached about the reaction going on inside her. Just the sound of his voice was enough to make giddy eddies of pleasure along her spine. It was incredible. How had he gotten her number? Should she ask?

"You're still angry." The warmth of humor shaded his inflection. "I wouldn't be surprised to learn that you'd taken out a contract on my life."

Georgianna tried to laugh but the sound caught in her throat.

"Hey, I'm only kidding," Maxim continued. "If you doubt my sincerity, put your husband on the line and I'll apologize to him."

"My husband isn't here," she said slowly, telling herself that unnecessary lies would make things worse.

Maxim squashed the spurt of pleasure that the information gave him. "I do apologize, Mrs. Manchester," he said, forcing himself to use her married name. "I didn't realize you were married until you pointed it out."

"I know," Georgianna admitted. "Let's just say it was one of those things." Good. Her voice sounded more friendly but reserved.

"You're still upset." It was a statement requiring no answer, so she didn't reply. "I'd like to give you the rocker. May I bring it by this afternoon?"

*The rocker.* Georgianna's spirits soared like a sky-rocket, only to plummet back to earth just as quickly. "I'm afraid I can't accept your generous offer, Mr. De Hoop. I can't afford to reimburse you for the price you paid. I was in over my head even before you started bidding against me."

Another nerve-stretching pause. "I certainly have a lot of strikes against me where you're concerned, don't I?"

Georgianna shrugged. "There'll be other fairs and other rockers."

"You wanted that rocker badly. Why?"

*Direct and aggressive,* she thought with a sinking feeling. She must be very careful. "I injured my back a few years ago. Sometimes it acts up. I thought the rocker might be soothing."

"I couldn't have made a worse impression if I'd tried."

Georgianna wasn't about to answer that statement. The kind of impression he'd made shouldn't have been made on a married woman. "Let's just say it wasn't meant to be, Mr. De Hoop."

"Maxim. And you must accept the rocker, as a gift

or as redress for grievances. Whichever will make you take it. I'll drop it by about four-thirty. See you then.''

Georgianna stared a moment at the silent receiver. Maxim 'Maxi-millions' De Hoop was dropping by at tea time. "Oh, brother!" she groaned and hung up.

The ring of the phone under her fingers should not have startled her, but it did.

"Did you take the phone off the hook?" demanded a very tense voice.

"Another call, Mr. Byrd," she volunteered dreamily.

"Maxim De Hoop," Alan murmured.

Georgianna jumped as though stuck by a pin. "Is this phone bugged? Well! Is it? If it is, I'm leaving town with no forwarding address."

"This is not some grade-B movie, Mrs. Manchester. We don't bug phones."

Alan sounded as disgusted with her as she was with herself. If Alan had been suspicious about her reaction to De Hoop before, now he must be quite certain that she was attracted to the man.

"Let's get this over with once and for all," Alan continued in his professional, neutral tone. "My research says De Hoop knows nothing more than you told him. He's after an attractive woman, that's all. So, I caution you to think over what you say to him. He's not on the alert, yet, but he's a professionally trained newspaper man. It won't take much to make him suspicious."

Georgianna sobered. "You're telling me not to have anything to do with him."

"Something like that. This isn't a game. We wouldn't have taken these precautions if we hadn't considered the situation potentially dangerous."

"I know." Georgianna tried to dispel the knot of fear that suddenly tightened her throat. "I won't do anything to embarrass you or endanger myself. I promise."

"Georgianna?" Alan's voice sounded a little tired, and for the first time she realized that he had probably been awake all night, working for her benefit. "De Hoop's a world-class jet-setter. Be careful. He may be the type to think nothing of pursuing a woman, wedding band or no."

She was grateful that he didn't add what was uppermost in both their minds. "I can handle myself, Alan. And if I can't, maybe you could come for a visit."

"As your big brother, you mean?"

"Something like that."

Alan chuckled and she knew she had made it back to firm ground yet again. "What will your neighbor think about your having a man staying with you?"

"If she doesn't believe you're my brother, we'll just have to confess the truth, that I'm an adulteress."

"Georgianna!"

"What a prude," she said laughingly. "Good-bye, Alan. And thank you. I say that a lot. I mean it."

"All in a day's work," he responded cheerfully, but when he had hung up she began to wonder just what sort of man Alan Byrd was. She'd never met him. He was only a voice on the phone.

"Oh, well, got to get ready for company!" she said aloud, and leaped out of bed.

"Why did I agree to this visit?" Georgianna moaned two hours later as she dusted the cocktail table. The very thought of being in close proximity with Maxim De Hoop did funny things to her breathing pattern. The man jangled her nerves and spun whirlwinds through her calm.

Of course, she hadn't actually agreed to see him. He'd taken the decision out of her hands. Alan wouldn't be pleased. He'd told her to stay away from De Hoop. But she wanted that chair, coveted it. And, if giving it to her would make De Hoop feel less guilty, she wasn't above taking it. It would be perfect in her bedroom, where she could rock and read to her heart's content.

Georgianna glanced at the stairway out in the foyer. Would De Hoop put it upstairs for her? Did she dare ask him? On the other hand, it was a big rocker. How would she ever get it upstairs if he didn't help?

She glanced at the fireplace. Wood. She would bring in some wood, start a fire, and then dash up and shower and change.

"Oh, murder!" The split logs in the cellar bin had been dwindling for days. She would have to chop kindling for a fire.

Ten minutes later she was in the backyard near the woodpile struggling with a hand axe which had become impossibly wedged in the end of a log.

"You're not cooperating!" she grumbled as she pounded the flat edge of the embedded axe with a hammer. The blade slid a fraction lower in the wood and the split widened slightly without freeing the axe.

"Having trouble?"

Georgianna thought of herself as a person who would never cringe. She was wrong. She recognized that voice. As if it wasn't too late to hide what she was doing, she swung the hammer and axe behind her back as she turned to face him. Maxim De Hoop. *Damn!*

He wore a sportscoat the shade of honey. Suede, she'd bet on it, though it was a seasonable fifty degrees. A burgundy tie, askew as though he had been jerking it, overlay a dark print shirt.

Maxim glanced at the splinters of wood on the ground beside her, the obvious carnage of her first, inept, attempts. He didn't laugh at her when she turned to him, but it was difficult not to. Wood chips clung to her sweater and her face was red with exertion. It was that funny, endearing jut of her chin, captured a dozen times on film, that made him not want to hurt her feelings.

"I'm early," he said as he bent to pick up the long-handled axe lying unused on the ground. The hand axe was still embedded in the half-split log. "I rang the bell, but there was no answer. Your neighbor told me I'd find you back here." He indicated the logpile. "I'll finish this job for you."

Georgianna didn't have the heart to glance at the logs she had so confidently laid out in anticipation of turning them into kindling.

"There's no need to do that," she said as he bent to pull a log from the pile. "I was really only wasting time."

"You shouldn't be out here at all, not with back

problems.'' He propped the bigger axe against the pile and started toward her, smiling now.

There was no dignity in hiding things behind one's back, she decided as he reached around her and took hold of her axe handle. His hand slid up until the edge of his palm just grazed hers and a tingle of pleasure shot through the full length of her arm. If only he wouldn't touch her.

His smile was magnetic up close. And it *was* close, only six inches from her face as he leaned near and said, ''Have you grown particularly fond of this particular log, Mrs. Manchester?''

Something flickered in the cerulean eyes watching her, and Georgianna wondered why she had to make such a big fool of herself when a small fool would do as well. He was watching her so intently, as if he was comparing her features against some standard, and she could only stare back in rapt fascination.

She realized she must have released the axe, because suddenly he began backing away from her, axe in hand. ''That's better, isn't it?''

She ignored the amusement in his gaze. ''I try to exercise a little each day, to stay limber.''

He laughed like he did everything else. It came suddenly, bursting full and free from the center of his being. Georgianna smiled. She liked it. She liked everything about the man. It was disgusting.

He walked across the grass to a stretch of driveway. Lifting the embedded axe, he brought the end of the log down hard on the concrete. A *crack* accompanied the impact, which split the log neatly in two, freeing the axe.

''This is for minor jobs,'' he said, waving the axe at

her. "You need the length and leverage of a full-sized axe for splitting logs. Let me show you."

"Not in those clothes," she protested.

He spread his arms to inspect himself. "I guess you're right. Here."

Georgianna was proud of herself for catching instead of dodging the axe that came slicing through the air. Actually, it came handle-up, a light toss with the blade down and away from her.

"You really . . . really . . . don't have . . . have to . . . Mr. De Hoop!" she protested as one after the other, his jacket, tie and, amazingly, his shirt followed the axe into her hands.

With a quick grin he walked over and picked up the wood axe. "Let's get to work."

Georgianna looked at the pile of clothing in her arms. The shirt was whispery soft. Silk. The buttery suede texture of his coat could only be chamois. When she looked up at him she didn't know what to think.

He wore no undershirt. Stripped to the waist he looked taller, broader than he seemed when dressed. And there was something else. He looked, well, less civilized. Many men looked naked—there was no other word for it—when they were unclothed. Maxim De Hoop looked at home, as if clothing were a concession to civilization that he would as soon do without.

And she understood why. The deep color of his face was no mere holiday tan. The deep bronzing went right down to where it disappeared into the waistband of his slacks.

She realized that she was staring yet again. No doubt

vanity made him strip before her to display those perfectly developed muscles.

*Too bad he looks so damn gorgeous,* she reflected. She would have liked to have been disdainful. Instead, she was growing unaccountably warm beneath the neckline of her sweater. "It's cold," she said in a lame effort at conversation.

Maxim smiled, as aware as she of her interested gaze. "On the Alaskan North Slope, this is considered summer weather. Anytime the thermometer rose above forty degrees, we'd strip completely and lie in the sun."

"I don't think Mrs. Walton would be amused," she answered, transferring her own reservations about what his next actions might be.

Maxim turned toward the neighboring yard and waved as though he saw someone. He was grinning like a boy when he turned back. "Do you think she's seen enough?"

"*I* sure have!" Georgianna murmured under her breath.

"If you insist on doing the manual labor, then I'm going inside to change," she called back over her shoulder, heading for her back steps. She couldn't just stand and watch him. "Knock when you've worn yourself out!"

The steamy heat of the shower was welcome. It helped ease the urgent pulse of blood that had begun the moment she'd heard his voice behind her. The pulsation had become a hammering as he undressed before her. She'd wanted to touch all that beautiful bare muscle, to feel its rippling warmth under her fingertips. And he knew it!

He was being deliberately provocative, despite his apology. It wasn't vanity that made her want to believe that. She'd looked at herself in the mirror every day for twenty-four years and knew her limitations for what they were. Too square a chin kept her from prettiness. She was too short and too healthy to attain a model willowiness. Nice but ordinary. Men didn't pant over her, at least not those whom she had hoped would. So, it must be that Maxim De Hoop was enjoying himself at her expense.

"Slumming," she murmured under her breath as she reached through the shower door for the bath sheet on the peg. Winding the terry cloth about her body, she stepped from the stall. She had no intention of becoming a dalliance for a bored millionaire, no matter how attractive a temptation he was.

Yet the sound of splitting wood drew her unhesitatingly to her bedroom window. Cautiously moving aside the curtain, she looked down into the yard below.

He was still working, the pile of neatly split logs larger than the untouched stack. As he bent to reach for another log, a fine film of perspiration gleamed like oil on the contoured surface of his back.

Georgianna's fingers flexed on the curtain, crushing its starched ruffle. Oh, but he was glorious to look at!

The fading sunlight made golden paths through the dark waves of his hair as he balanced a log on the stump he had been using as a platform. Muscles bunched beneath the skin of his back and arms as he raised the axe in a graceful arch and brought it down in the middle of the standing log. A solid *whack!* sounded a scant second before the log fell into two parts to the ground.

He might be a wealthy playboy, but he handled the axe as though he'd worked with it all his life, she conceded. No wonder he was in such good shape. His muscles were hardened and toughened by physical labor. Yet how was that possible?

"Maybe he chops wood to impress all his lady-friends," she said to herself and then laughed at the absurdity of the remark.

The rustle of the curtain must have caught his attention, because he looked up suddenly, straight at her window. Afraid that any move would give away her spying, Georgianna froze until his head turned to his work once more. He hadn't seen her . . . she hoped.

Fifteen minutes later she'd slipped on her favorite dolman-sleeve sweater of jade green and a pair of black wool slacks. Before the mirror she had outlined her eyes with a slate-colored pencil and brushed on a smoky shadow that enhanced them and gave them depth. Finally, she hesitated over her choice of perfume. A weakness of hers, the newest purchase was an exotic fragrance meant for nighttime encounters full of promise. Good sense overruled temptation and she chose a light woodsy fragrance.

"You can come in now," she called from her kitchen door a minute later.

"Almost done!" came his rejoinder.

She hesitated a moment, staring at him through the screen as she gnawed a corner of her lip. She'd feel like a fool standing and watching him until he was done. Besides, that would only encourage him in whatever game he was playing.

*Might as well finish preparing dinner*, she decided,

and turned back to the kitchen. To go with the whole-wheat rolls she was baking, she'd been simmering a pot of split peas all day. They were thick and stiff now, ready to be rubbed through a sieve before being thinned with milk to make soup.

She'd just poured a part of the mixture into the colander and begun rubbing it through the tiny holes with a wooden spoon when the back door opened.

"Whew! I could go for a beer now!" He stood in the doorway, holding an armful of wood. Brushing a trickle of sweat from his brow with the back of one hand, he grinned at her. His eyes made a lazy perusal of her as he leaned a naked shoulder against the doorjamb. "I'll bet you don't drink beer."

"No," Georgianna replied, looking away. She'd never have expected beer to be to his taste either. "But I think there's something similar in the butler's pantry. English ale or something, next to the wine rack. Help yourself." She used the handle of the spoon to point out the direction. "I put your things in the living room. Feel free to use the bathroom. First door on the right at the top of the stairs."

She heard him call "All right!" in satisfied tones before he stuck his head back into the kitchen for an instant, waving a brown bottle. "My compliments to your husband when he arrives."

"Husband?" Georgianna murmured when he was gone. Of course, he probably thought this was her home and that her husband was coming home for dinner.

She paused, staring unseeingly at the colander. What would he do or say when he found out that there was no husband coming home tonight, or any night? Well, she wasn't about to inform him of that fact.

A few minutes later water began to flow in the upstairs bath, a heavy rush into the tub that could only mean one thing. "Maxi-millions" was taking a shower. Why would he do that when he expected her husband to show up at any moment? Didn't he know how it would look? Or, maybe he didn't care. Maybe he thought it would be great fun to embarrass her and upset her husband. The few times she'd seen him, he'd shown a remarkable disregard for propriety or the feelings of others. Evidently Mr. De Hoop believed that money gave one special privileges.

"Insufferable man!" She pushed the last of the peas through the colander with her spoon, then burst into infectious laughter. Perhaps she could teach Mr. De Hoop a lesson in manners.

It was easy to set a beautiful table. Linen and crystal were whisked from their places and laid out. She added a pair of silver candelabras with white tapers to bracket the silver bowl of late-fall rosebuds she had placed on the table earlier in the day. At each end of the long elegant dining room table she set a place. Finally she set a place off-center, the knife and fork not quite straight, as if added as an afterthought.

In the living room she started a fire, placed two snifters and the brandy decanter on a silver tray beside the sofa, and then placed a slow jazzy album on the turntable. Once the lights were turned down, the warmth of the newly lit fire gave a shadowy seductive glow to the room.

Hands on hips, she surveyed her work. Only a clod would miss the implications of the candlelight and brandy. And the wide expanse of white fur . . . well, the possibilities were obvious. Private party for two, she and her husband. He was obviously an unwelcome third wheel. With luck she wouldn't have to say a word.

By the time the soup was simmering with the additions of milk and sherry, she was almost eager for him to come downstairs. A few minutes after the shower had stopped, she'd heard the high whine of her hair dryer. He did make himself at home.

"Come on," she murmured as she pushed the first pan of rolls into the oven. It was not quite five-thirty, a little early for a husband to return from a grueling day at the office, but that didn't matter. She expected her guest to be gone before the point came up.

"Decent again!"

His shirt slung over his shoulder, Maxim wore only his slacks, his well-proportioned chest still on display. Gazing at him, Georgianna was conscious again of an abrupt change in her heart rate. He looked untamed, supremely male, predatory.

"Come in and have a seat," she suggested stiffly, annoyed beyond reason by his engaging smile. *Why didn't he have the self-conscious need to put on a shirt?* Did he really think she would whistle and stomp in response to his striptease?

"What do you do for a living, Mr. De Hoop?"

The question just leaped out but she discovered it was a perfect way to disconcert him. When she glanced up, there was a look of simple surprise on his face.

"You haven't lived in Plowden long," he observed as

he swung a leg over a stool before the counter on which she worked.

"Not long," she agreed, keeping her eyes on the fruit salad she was preparing.

"Do you read the newspaper?"

Any other time she'd have responded to the quiet warning tone in his voice. But he was just a little too smug about himself to suit her.

"Hardly ever," she said airily. "Never the local sort, certainly. They seem to be nothing but grocery ads held together by leftover bits of newswire stories nobody else is interested in printing."

The fractional silence was too much to bear. "Would you care for another ale?" she asked politely, and looked up.

She was amazed by the anger in his face, surprised all the more because she was certain the anger was not directed at her. "Did I say something wrong?" she ventured anyway.

A mischievous gleam came into his eyes. "Hardly. The truth is the truth is the truth."

She shrugged. "I won't even begin to puzzle that out. You will stay for dinner, won't you? Edward and I never do anything fancy. It's just soup, salad, and homemade bread, but there's plenty."

His eyelids flickered, a sweep of black lashes touching his tan cheeks, and then a triumphant grin settled on his features. "I'd be delighted."

She nodded, not trusting her voice. There was no hesitation in his answer; no 'Are you certain your husband won't mind?'; no 'I couldn't possibly intrude on such short notice.' He had gotten what he wanted, an invitation to spend more time in her home. But why did he want it?

"Shall I start your fire?"

Again Georgianna found herself staring into glorious blue eyes bright with amusement. Light her fire, indeed! As if she would let him. "I started it myself. I'm quite capable of looking after myself."

"I believe you," he answered warmly. Then, in a lower register, "But sometimes the best things are those that are shared."

"Edward would agree," she returned with a coy smile. His face went blank. The smile annoyed him, she realized. Or perhaps it was the mention of her husband's name. De Hoop was flirting with her and he didn't like the idea of her being reminded of her husband.

*Too bad!*

"Would you mind checking the blaze, after all? I really didn't do more than make certain the kindling caught."

When he disappeared into the hallway, Georgianna released a sigh that lifted the feathery bangs across her brow. Talk about nerve! She'd insulted a millionaire publisher and gotten away with it. Of course, he thought she didn't know who he was. She smiled. She had no intention of enlightening him.

It didn't take long. In two minutes, he was back. The first and only thing she noticed before he spoke was that his shirt was on and half-buttoned. "How long have you been married?"

It was an ordinary question, but the tone was purely combative.

"Not long. Less than two months," Georgianna answered, the mystified look on her face genuine.

"Is today some sort of special occasion?" There was a frown on his face.

"When you're married only two months, every day is special." The huskiness of her voice added not-so-subtle meaning to the words. He'd seen the arrangements in the living room and had taken the hint.

Maxim's frown deepened. "Your husband must be very successful for you to own such a lovely home so soon."

She smiled serenely. "We're fortunate for our age, Mr. De Hoop."

He had the grace to blush. An unexpected shade of red mottled the high ridge of each cheek as he said, "Stupid of me to inquire. I apologize."

He glanced at his watch, an expensive hunk of gold that she hadn't noticed earlier when he sat across from her. Fifteen thousand dollars if it cost a penny, she'd thought. Yet it served the same function as thousands of other, cheaper, watches. "Hell! I forgot. I'm late for an appointment."

His eyes didn't quite meet hers as he stuffed his shirt into his slacks. "I won't be able to stay, after all. Give my respects to your husband. Another time, perhaps."

"Certainly," Georgianna answered, offering no other date. "About the rocker—"

"I placed it on the front porch before I came in. I'm really late. Sorry."

Georgianna followed his hurried stride back into the living room, where he picked up his coat and then continued into the front hall. Only then did he turn to her and hold out his hand.

She couldn't refuse. Begrudgingly she held out her hand to have it clasped in a startlingly firm grasp. She looked up at him and knew too late that that was a mistake.

For a long moment they stood staring at one another and there was desire in their gazes. It communicated itself with the same intensity as a physical touch. The voluptuous sensation enveloped her and she didn't resist, for this would be all they would ever know. In the dim recesses of her mind where rationality had fled, she thought it strange that his touch could so overwhelm her. For an instant she seemed to lean toward him, drawn by a will greater than her own. The next her hand was released and the chasm between them split wide.

"Good-bye, Mrs. Manchester."

"Good-bye, Mr. De Hoop."

The ringing of the phone came an hour later, long after the soup had boiled over and the whole-wheat rolls had burned.

"Mrs. Manchester?"

"Alan? If you've dug up some dirt on 'Maxi-millions', I'm not interested."

"Georgianna, I've got some news. It's not good. In fact, it's what we feared. Let me start at the beginning."

# *Chapter Six*

*I*t was three A.M.. The glow from a streetlamp poured through the open window. The sheer curtains danced in the yellow beam of light on the chilly fall breeze. It was cold. The neighbors had shut their windows and drawn the drapes against the night air. None of them felt terrified, suffocated by the night's darkness.

Lying wide-eyed on her bed, still dressed in sweater and slacks, Georgianna stared at the ceiling. She'd thought this would be a lark, a kind of make-believe espionage for adults. She'd never thought of herself as really being in any danger. She'd even suggested her own alias: Mrs. Edward Manchester. As a married woman she would seem more respectable and stable. It was a game. A safety precaution like the old adage about an ounce of prevention. But now, suddenly, the game was over. The need for safety was very real.

Protective custody, that was what the Justice Department had called the procedure. She would only be away from home for a few weeks or months, until the trial began. She was a key witness for the government. They didn't want her getting cold feet or being harassed. Her testimony was crucial.

It was simply going to be a kind of extended holiday. They would settle matters with her employers. Her job would be waiting when she returned. There'd be nothing to worry about if she kept the right attitude, kept her perspective, and her sense of humor.

So, she'd agreed to be sent to Plowden, Connecticut, where Alan Byrd became her lifeline. It was essential that no friends or family know her whereabouts. She'd even nixed the idea of telling her parents, though they were out of the country. She didn't want to worry them.

Innocent bystander. How often she'd read and heard those words in news accounts of a crime. She'd always felt sorry for the hapless soul who happened to be in the wrong place at the wrong time. It never occurred to her that she might one day be the innocent bystander. But two months ago that was just what had happened.

Georgianna squeezed her lids closed as fresh tears stung her already red eyes.

She was just starting her career as a lawyer, having passed her law boards in the spring, and was working for the local Legal Aid office. Was her overzealousness to blame?

Estacio Gonzales had skipped on his parole officer before. As often as not, he would show up a day late, smiling that sensuous smile that had half the girls on

Stateline Street vying for his attention. With his dark Latin looks and his macho swagger, he had possessed a tough urban charm far beyond his fifteen years. Yet his smile was as sweet as honey, warm and golden, especially for any female. The first time she met Estacio, he had accompanied his mother to her office to discuss difficulties with their landlord. He didn't speak, but she had noticed his encouraging smile whenever his mother glanced at him.

The second time they met, at a local police station, she couldn't believe that he'd been accused of killing a thug in a knife fight. Not this boy with the sweet-as-sugar smile.

But, facing him across the short distance of a cell a few minutes later, she'd begun to believe. The smile had disappeared, his expression becoming cool and remote when she had asked why he had killed the boy.

He'd shrugged, the sinewy muscles of his shoulders and arms half exposed by a torn sweat shirt. "He called my mother a—" and he reeled off a string of Spanish profanities that Georgianna hadn't understood nor cared to. She did understand that Estacio loved his mother and had responded to those insults as the law of the streets dictated: with violence.

He had been lucky. He was a minor and, with no prior offenses against him, was back on the streets after two months in a juvenile hall.

At first he was on time for his meetings at the legal aid office. Then he began to skip. He had a job, but Georgianna doubted that he was earning enough to pay for his new and flashy wardrobe. Yet the new brightness in his onyx-black gaze disturbed her more. She suspected that he'd succumbed to the panacea for poverty in the ghetto: drugs.

That was why she'd gone looking for him when he didn't show for two days after a missed parole meeting. She had his home address. She'd decided to drop by after work for a friendly chat. Estacio was not at home.

She hadn't counted on getting a flat tire that she could not change because of her back. A woman in his building had pointed out a hallway phone. After calling a garage, she'd gone back to her car and waited.

City streets can be lonely at night, especially a side street. Not many people passed her after the first hour.

When a vehicle finally turned onto the street, she'd sighed in gratitude. But it had not been from the garage. The two men that got out entered Estacio's building. After a moment, she climbed out of her car to make another call. The garage man hadn't come. It was time to call a friend.

"Stupid, stupid," Georgianna murmured. Looking back, she could see it was a stupid thing to do. She could have been mugged, raped, or both. But she'd become worried at finding herself stranded in that area so late at night.

The moment she entered the hallway she knew she'd made a grave error. The naked bulb spotlighted the two men and a third party. In the split second when she saw the three faces she'd known she'd never forget them. The exchanged bundles hadn't needed labels. She'd stumbled upon a drug deal.

She saw the gun in one man's hand, saw the blinding

flash, and heard the deafening report that shoved the third man back against the brick wall.

She hadn't realized that she was running until the cool metallic surface of her car hood met her outstretched hands. The second shot shattered the windshield of her car and she threw herself forward, past the bumper and into the gutter.

The sound of police sirens had seemed like a dream. Even when she was lifted from the street, she had screamed and fought until the officer's brusque voice forced reality on her.

Georgianna drew in several hiccuping breaths of air. She felt as though she were drowning in the memory, the terror of that night not quite two months ago. She was safe, she told herself. Safe.

The murder victim had been an undercover man for the Justice Department. For nearly a year the authorities had been trying to get evidence on the two drug dealers who were arrested that night. Now they were caught, and her testimony as a witness to murder would put them behind bars for life.

She was a perfect witness, the authorities had assured her. She was smart, an attorney. Without hesitation she had picked the men out of a lineup. They had an airtight case against them with her cooperation.

She'd never thought of refusing to testify. The news of Estacio's death from a drug overdose less than a week after her ordeal had strengthened her resolve to see justice done. The scum that profited from the hopeless desperation of people like Estacio must be eradicated.

One of the accused had been immediately eligible for

release on bail. The six-figure bond would have kept most petty criminals in jail. The fact that the man was free within an hour of the posting of the bond meant only one thing. The men had connections, high connections with organized crime. Whoever had paid the bond money hoped that he would get his money's worth. That was when the authorities suggested that she leave town for the few months before the trial.

"But it's not so simple anymore," she whispered to herself. Alan Byrd's phone call had destroyed her peace, her safe haven. The government agents had lost track of the suspect, whom they'd been tailing since his release.

Georgianna sat up suddenly, hugging her arms as her teeth began to chatter. She'd refused Alan's suggestion that she give up her place in Plowden for protective custody. She didn't want to share a hotel room with a police woman until the man was found. For better or worse, she had done all the running she meant to do.

Alan had warned her to be extra careful, to keep to herself. But what he hadn't said was more frightening than the rest. She was no fool. The freed man was looking for her, to make certain that she would not be able to testify against him. Her life was in danger.

"Oh, God!"

Sweat trickled down her forehead, but her hands and feet felt like blocks of ice. Her body shivered uncontrollably as she curled into a tight ball atop her bedspread. She had heard about anxiety attacks, but the knowledge did not help. Panic was welling up inside her, clawing at the back of her raw throat until she thought she would begin to scream.

She jumped inside her skin as the phone jangled to life on her bedstand.

Two. Three rings.

She stared at it in the dark as though it was a coiled black snake ready to strike if she reached out an unprotected hand. What if it were that man?

Four. Five rings.

She tried to move her hand toward it but her muscles were locked in fright.

Seven. Eight rings.

"Dear Lord, make it go away!"

Ten. Eleven . . .

Silence.


"I'm coming! I'm coming!" Georgianna called as she shuffled down the front stairs. Whoever dared to ring her doorbell before seven A.M. was going to get a piece of her mind, she told herself stoutly, trying to quell her fear. After belting her robe over the clothes she had slept in, she peered through the door's peephole.

Cora stood on her steps, a coat thrown over her robe.

"Come in, it's freezing!" Georgianna exclaimed when she had thrown wide the door. "What's the matter, Cora? Has something happened?"

"That's my question to you." Cora's sharp-eyed gaze took in Georgianna's swollen eyes and tousled hair. "Are you sick?" She put a cool hand to the younger woman's flushed cheek. "You look simply awful and you feel feverish. When I noticed your lights in the middle of the night, I wondered if something was wrong. When you didn't answer the phone, I nearly came over."

"You called last night? What time was it?"

Cora patted her cheek. "Didn't wake you, did I? I thought as much. When I didn't see any lights in the upstairs bath or bedroom, I decided that you must be a heavy sleeper. I'd have been sound asleep at three-thirty myself except I had forgotten to turn on the heater out in the greenhouse. Shot up in bed like a bolt when I remembered. But now, let's see about you. Have you had an upset stomach, chills, or such?"

"You called." Georgianna felt like a weight had been lifted from her. But what lights could she have left on? A glance at the living room gave her the answer. Both table lamps were burning. "I—I guess I fell asleep without my final room check," she murmured when she turned back to Cora. "I'm sorry if I worried you. It was good of you to come and check on me."

"Nonsense." Cora smiled. "First thing for you to do is climb back in bed while I make you a cup of tea. Your hands are like ice, dear. You must try to rest. I'll call my doctor's office promptly at nine."

Georgianna shook her head. "No, please don't. I'm fine. Really. I just had a bad night. I can take care of myself."

Cora's gaze narrowed again and Georgianna racked her brain for an explanation. After all, the woman barely knew her. She might begin to suspect all kinds of things. At best, she would probably inform the Rhoadses that the person they had hired to house-sit was not very reliable. A change of location was the last thing she wanted to deal with at the moment.

Georgianna bent her head suddenly, hoping that she would be forgiven for yet another lie. "I—I heard from

Edward last night. He called from somewhere in the Mediterranean. I guess I miss him more than I thought. I cried myself to sleep afterward."

"My *dear*," Cora crooned as she enfolded Georgianna in her arms. "Poor, poor girl. Of course you miss your young man."

Georgianna, accepting this mothering with a guilty conscience, resolved to come back and explain everything to Cora when her ordeal was over. She had never been a good liar and the fact that she must trick so kindhearted a soul made her doubly ashamed.

"Now you go straight back up those stairs and get some rest," Cora directed, turning Georgianna about by the shoulders. "The last thing your husband would want is for you to make yourself sick over his absence. When you're feeling up to it you can come over for a cup of coffee and tell me about your visit with Mr. De Hoop."

Georgianna sighed inwardly. This woman didn't miss a trick. As she went back upstairs after closing the door behind her neighbor, she decided that bed was the only place to be.

Maybe it was Cora's early-morning visit, or perhaps it was just the soothing light of day, but when the phone awakened Georgianna at half past ten, she reached for it without a second thought.

"You lied to me!"

Drugged by deep sleep, Georgianna yawned broadly. "This must be 'Maxi-millions' De Hoop. I don't know which lie you're talking about and, frankly, I couldn't care less. Leave me alone, Mr. De Hoop, or I'll set the authorities on you!"

She heard him bark, "I'll be there in ten minutes!"

just before the receiver landed in its cradle. Ten seconds later she was snoring peacefully under a pile of pillows.


"Well? Aren't you going to open the door?"

Georgianna peered one-eyed through the peephole in astonishment. A very determined-looking Maxim De Hoop was on her doorstep just as he had promised.

"Go away!" she ordered through the barrier of the door.

"Open the door, Mrs. Manchester, or I'm going to make a spectacle all your neighbors should enjoy," he threatened.

"I'm going to call my husband," Georgianna shouted. Another lie. Oh well, this was no time to stop.

There was a short pause. The words, when they came, were loud and distinct. "You have no husband to call. This is not your home. You, Mrs. Manchester, are an imposter!"

Georgianna stiffened. He'd found her out! Her fingers curled about the doorknob as she braced herself to face him. There was nothing to do but brave it out.

When she opened the door he was standing with one hand braced on the doorframe above his head. She barely noticed that he wore no tie and that his hair was mussed. What she did notice was the madder-than-blue-blazes look on his face.

Her own anger leaped at the sight of him.

"I don't know how you found out and I don't care. All I want to know is what you're planning to do about it."

The barrage of words seemed to catch Maxim off-guard and a little of the anger faded from his face, but his tone was belligerent all the same. "What do you suggest I do?"

She lifted her chin. "I suggest that you go away and forget we ever met. A decent man wouldn't . . . wouldn't . . ." In horror she heard her voice crack. Oh, no! The last thing she must do is cry in front of him. What a story that would make for his paper. "Go away!"

He caught the door in his hand, preventing her from shutting it in his face. "Just a minute." He forced her and the door back as he entered the hall. "I don't know why, but I feel you owe me an explanation. Why all the need for this charade?"

Georgianna remained behind the open door, holding it to her shoulder as though it were a shield against his anger.

"Charade?" she voiced scornfully. "Just what would you call that little number you pulled at the county fair? Did you really think I'd be so dumb as to believe that you were overwhelmed by my great beauty? You were after something, Mr. De Hoop. At first I didn't realize what it was."

Georgianna continued despite his look of skepticism. "Didn't you stop to think that someone might point out who you were? Oh, yes, I know who you are. I've known for days. Mr. Maxim De Hoop, millionaire publisher, owner of a string of newspapers from Maine to Georgia. As if that should give you special privilege. Not with me, Mr. De Hoop. Not with me. I'm not interested in anything you have to offer."

He folded his arms across his chest, watching her now

with frank cynicism. "If what you say is true then my memory must be faulty. I don't recall your refusing my kiss in the park the other day. And I sure as hell didn't imagine your unconcealed interest in my . . . physique yesterday."

The deliberate pause was an attempt to insult her, and it did. Georgianna's mouth formed an angry 'O' of affront, but Maxim was too annoyed to stop. "I can read the signs when a woman's interested. But you, lady, have been giving out enough signals to confuse the best."

"Was I supposed to fall for you before or after I gave you the story you're looking for?" Her voice rose from its husky register to an indignant soprano. "You arrogant bastard!"

Maxim gave his head a quick, angry shake. "Don't confuse the issue. If you weren't as interested in me as I was in you, I wouldn't be here now. And don't make the mistake of thinking it was only a harmless flirtation we've been engaging in."

He took a step toward her. "I don't participate in that adolescent sport any longer." A second step brought him within arm's length of her. "I play hardball, Mrs. Manchester."

"Amoral! Unethical! Don't try to hide behind your charm. We both know what you've been after from the first. I didn't want to believe that you were that unscru-pulous, so eager to get what you wanted, that you would stoop to . . . to . . . Well, the answer's no. N–O. No! Is that perfectly clear?"

"I came for answers and I'm going to get them!" he shouted back.

Georgianna shook her head, but she couldn't speak. She felt like she'd been repeatedly kicked until her insides hurt. She'd suspected from the beginning that Maxim De Hoop was a newspaper man on the trail of an exclusive story. But now that he was openly admitting as much to her, it made her sick and she couldn't even say why. It didn't matter. What mattered was whether her cover could be salvaged despite his discovery. She had to know what he planned to do with his new knowledge.

Without looking up, she said, "How did you find out about me?"

Maxim sighed, the last of his anger dwindling as he searched for words that would not make him sound like a man obsessed. For that was what he was, obsessed with this unattainable woman. She'd played with him, probably laughed at him behind his back. Just the thought of it made him angry all over again.

He glanced quickly at her. Her eyes were still downcast and the slender fingers clutching the door were bloodless with tension.

"I found out about you by accident. My secretary looked up your number for me the first time. I found out that you weren't listed and didn't have time to track it down myself. After I got home last night, I decided to call you."

When Georgianna raised surprised eyes to meet his sardonic blue gaze, he growled, "Gullible fool that I am, I thought you and your husband might enjoy being my guests at a dinner party the *Plowden Chronicle* is hosting next week. I didn't have your number with me, so I called Cora Walton. In the course of the conversation, she told me what you had gone to great lengths to hide."

Georgianna's jaw dropped. What was he talking about? Cora Walton knew nothing about her situation. "Cora told you? Told you what?"

Maxim's contempt reasserted itself. "That this is not your home, for one. Did you think you could impress me by lying about that?" He glanced about the hallway. "It's charming, but hardly in the same league with some places I've known." His gaze came back, sliding over her terry-cloth robe with pointed interest. "You, on the other hand, are in a league by yourself."

"Oh no, you don't!" Georgianna released the door and sent it slamming shut. "Keep your sarcasm to yourself. Finish telling me what Cora told you. Now."

Annoyance wrinkled his brow. "Must we stand in the hall? It's freezing now that you've let the heat out."

"I didn't invite you in," she reminded him, the jut of her chin defiant.

"No, you didn't," he answered in a deceptively gentle voice. "But you did yesterday. You let me in and you very nearly let me into your bed, didn't you?"

Georgianna stopped breathing when his hand touched her face. Dangerous; he looked very, very dangerous. Then she felt his forefinger trace the half-moon scar on her cheek.

"You got cold feet, didn't you, Georgie?" His was a whispered purr of a voice. "You had time to think while I was upstairs showering. You were thinking, 'I'm a married woman. What if my husband finds out when he returns from sea duty? What if someone tells him?' That's what made you pretend that your husband was living here with you, wasn't it?"

His finger continued its mesmerizing motion on the

satin-soft skin of her cheek. "Was the brandy and fire really meant for us, Georgie? Had you imagined what it would be like for the two of us to lie side by side before that warm blaze?" He moved nearer until his breath eddied across the surface of her face. "Did you wonder what it would be like to lie naked in my arms? To be made love to on the fur rug?"

"If you try to kiss me again, I'll bite you."

For a moment she thought he would kiss her anyway. But then he moved back, his hand leaving her face. He shook his head slowly as if he, too, could not quite believe what had just occurred.

*He knows nothing, nothing at all!*

The realization hit her all at once. He knew nothing about her, the murder she'd witnessed, or that she was in hiding. He was only a bored playboy interested in seducing a lonely married woman. Indignation replaced her relief, swamping her with the desire to strike him.

"You want facts, Mr. De Hoop, I'll give you facts," she said tightly, not bothering to hide her hostility as she advanced toward him. "My husband is a naval officer on a tour of duty aboard a submarine. I am house-sitting for a couple named Rhoads. Is that what you came to hear me say? Oh, there's something more."

Her hands bunched into fists as she remembered his nasty suggestion that she had panted over him. "I know this may come as something of a blow, but I find you totally resistible. If I were tempted to be unfaithful, the least I would expect in my lover is tact, gentleness, and genuine human warmth. That lets you out on all three counts!"

Maxim stared at her. He was confused, irritated, and

fascinated all at once. He had expected her to prevaricate, to try to excuse herself for the sham she had perpetrated. He had expected her to deny, but then ultimately admit, her interest in him. She had led him on. Lord knew she had! That was the only explanation for the desire that heaved inside him every time he saw her. *She* had led *him* on . . . hadn't she?

He moved another step away from her, repelled by the anger radiating from her like heat. She was furious. But there was something else behind the blaze of anger, something almost, but not quite, hidden. When he'd first confronted her, she had looked . . . cornered.

Yes, Maxim thought, she'd looked as though he had discovered something about her that was much more serious than the dissemblings of an unfaithful wife.

*Get hold of yourself,* he commanded himself. He'd done a great deal too much speculating about Georgianna Manchester, and none of it to his credit.

"I'm cold," Georgianna said finally, hugging her body with her arms. "If you're finished with me . . ."

He meant to simply leave. He was already walking toward the door, toward her, when she uttered that final line of challenge. He couldn't resist.

He held her chin gently between his thumb and forefinger. "I'll go, but I'm not finished with you, Georgie. Not by a long shot!"

# Chapter Seven

$\mathcal{T}$his is very kind of you, dear," Cora Walton said as she poured a stream of golden tea into two eggshell-thin Balleek cups. "Frank has been scolding me for months about my column. He says it's too technical, too dry." Chuckling, she placed a tea cosy over the pot. "I told him there is nothing technical about violets, but he made me promise to let a friend preview my column this time. I thought of you immediately, because you've helped me in the greenhouse."

Georgianna looked up from the article she'd been reading, entitled "The Care and Propagation of African Violets." After a week of solitude, Cora's call for help had come as welcome relief.

"I'm flattered, Cora, but I don't know what I can do. This sounds straightforward to me. The only thing I would suggest is that you use the common names of plants. For instance—'' She pointed to the second paragraph—''this column is about the different leaf forms and color range. You write about *Saintpaulia ionantha* and *Saintpaulia grotei*. Personally, I wouldn't have the nerve to purchase a plant that sounds like it has a better pedigree than I do.''

Cora leaned forward, her half-lens glasses sliding down her nose. ''I see. Names like Bluejean and Springtime Sweetheart are more friendly.''

''Exactly,'' Georgianna replied. ''When you talk to me about your plants, you call them by name. If I were you, I might think about changing the tone of your article to sound more like a conversation. I'm always fascinated by your astounding knowledge of plant life. You could even change the name of the column. You know the sort of thing, 'Cora's Babies on Parade.' '' Georgianna stopped abruptly. ''Brother! For somebody who said she had no suggestions, I've just completely revamped your article. Sorry.''

''No, no.'' Cora peered over her glasses, a beatific smile brightening her face. ''It's perfect! Perfect. I don't know why I didn't realize the trouble before.'' She took the pages from Georgianna and dropped them in the wastebasket. ''I've two hours before I have to deliver a column to Frank's office. Do you think we can do a new one before lunch?''

Georgianna laughed. ''If you think we can, I don't know why not. After all, I don't have to do any of the work.''

Cora went in search of pen and paper. Instead, she returned with a portable typewriter and a sheepish smile.

"Do you type, dear? I've never quite gotten the hang of it. It took me four hours to type those two mistake-free pages."

An hour and three cups of tea later, Georgianna typed "The End," finishing the new column. "I like it," she pronounced after a final perusal.

"So do I." Cora beamed down at her. "You're an absolute wonder, Georgianna. Sixty words per minute. I'm terribly impressed. I'm amazed you didn't seek employment as a secretary rather than deciding to house-sit."

"I was looking for a temporary kind of job."

Georgianna slipped the typewriter back into its case. At least she hadn't had to think up that answer. Alan Byrd had suggested the job for the same reason. She'd asked for permission to find employment, but had been told she couldn't look for a job that would require references because that would alert friends or employers to where she'd gone. When Alan had suggested this job as a house-sitter, she had jumped at it.

"Would you like to ride down to the *Chronicle* with me? Afterward we can stop at a fish-and-chips place I know. Lunch is the least I can do to repay you for your help."

Georgianna rose to her feet. "No, not today, Cora. Just look at the time! I've got a million things to do. Thanks all the same." She didn't look up, unable to face Cora's hurt expression. Dammit, anyway! She wasn't supposed to socialize much. Certainly she didn't want to go to the *Chronicle*'s offices, where she might run into Maxim De Hoop. No thank you. She couldn't face that.

"Will you come back for dinner then? I'm making

Boston baked beans. Even though I halved the recipe, there's enough for ten people.''

Georgianna nodded. "I'd be delighted."

"By the way," Cora put in as Georgianna was about to leave, "are you coming to the dinner dance at the *Chronicle?* I know Maxim invited you."

Georgianna shook her head emphatically. "Your company I would enjoy. De Hoop's I can do without."

A few minutes later, Georgianna slammed the front door as she marched into her home.

Massaging her throbbing temples with one hand, she slumped down on the third step of the hall stairway. "Rats!" The strain was beginning to tell on her. The seven days and seven nights of solitude since De Hoop's last visit had strung her nerves to their limits. It took all her effort to sound normal and content when Alan called each evening. The morning with Cora had helped, but not much.

A sudden ominous roar in the basement shot her to her feet until she realized that it was just the heater coming to life.

"How an I supposed to last another two months?" she muttered wearily as she subsided onto the step.

It would be at least January before the trial date was set. The defense lawyers were using every trick in the book. Perhaps if she hadn't been a lawyer herself, she would have been more consoled by Alan's guarantee that she wouldn't have to stay in hiding much longer. Motions for delay and other tactics could set the trial date back for years!

She leaned her head against the railing post. She hadn't had a good night's sleep in a week. Even changing beds had not helped. The pile of books she'd brought with her were all unread. She'd even given up teaching herself to cook. Music was her only solace. If she gave in to the fears that nibbled at her she would be a basket case long before the trial.

The grand proportions of this house had once seemed the epitome of luxury. Now the house was simply too big for her peace of mind. A week ago she'd locked the door at the bottom of the steps leading to the third floor, after having checked and relocked every window. To her chagrin, she found she couldn't force herself to go into the basement after dark. In fact, she'd placed a kitchen chair under the locked doorknob of the basement door.

"So what am I going to do?" she murmured, rubbing her cheek against the smooth wood. Her nerves simply couldn't stand much more of this paranoia. She was starting at shadows, shying at make-believe dragons in the basement, frightening herself out of all proportion to the reality of the menace. Just because the agents had lost track of their man, it didn't follow that the criminal was on her trail.

"Maybe I'll go to a movie tomorrow night," she said aloud, feeling better at just the thought of activity. Alan had warned her not to become chummy with anyone, but he hadn't said she couldn't go out at all.

Tomorrow she would start in on her cooking again, and make a list of things she could do without drawing attention to herself. The chances of being found far from home, in a state where she had no friends or relatives or connections of any kind, were quite remote. With a little forethought she should be able to go about as much as she wanted to. There was the library, open late every other night. And the beach. She hadn't been to the beach since the day at Fairfield Bay.

Georgianna sucked in a quick angry breath at the thought of Maxim De Hoop. That was one emotion she had no desire to banish. Just the thought of him raised the hackles on her neck. He'd called her a flirt, a tease, tried to blame her for his lust.

She'd met a few sore losers in her life, but De Hoop took the cake. At least he would never have any idea how close he'd come to a news scoop.

The thought cheered her considerably. He wasn't as sharp or savvy as he liked to think. "So much for the trained mind of a professional newspaperman," she scoffed.

Still, it would have been nice to think that a man like that was really interested in her.

"Oh no, you don't, Georgianna Helton! You're not to feel sorry for yourself anymore today. When this is over, maybe you will sweep Alan Byrd off his feet!"

Laughing, she stood up. Her anxiety hadn't subsided completely, but at least she'd admitted that she was ashamed of herself for the spiritless way she'd behaved. She could have backed out of this months ago. Now there were people depending on her, and she had no intention of letting them down.

She would take a long hot bath, dress in something that would lift her spirits, and then go over to Cora Walton's house and enjoy herself.

"Why this way, Max?" his date queried as she reached across the space between the custom seats of the

Lamborghini and linked her arm through his. She peered out in puzzlement at the quiet residential street swathed in late-fall mist, recognizing it as Quaker Lane. "We've been out every night this week and you always bring me home this way when you know it would be shorter if we took a through street."

Maxim turned his head briefly from the street to smile at his stunning dinner partner. "Maybe I just want to be in your company a little longer, Steph. Taking the long way home gives me that chance."

Encouraged by his high-wattage smile, Stephanie Brayton angled her body toward his, wrapping a second arm about his. "You could be in my company a great deal longer, if you want it. Say you'll come in tonight, Max. It's only nine o'clock and I've a bottle of champagne chilling," she suggested softly.

Maxim said nothing, but turned and quickly kissed her on the cheek. Why, indeed, should he not accept the invitation? He and Stephanie were old, if not intimate, friends. During the summer he and she had turned eighteen, his mother and hers had entertained hopes of a match between their children. But at eighteen Maxim had been no competition for the aristocratic wiles of Arne Bergsling, the twenty-five-year-old Norwegian heir to a shipbuilding fortune. It was the marriage of the season that year in Connecticut, but it lasted less than two years. Since then, Stephanie had been in turn Mrs. Phillip Worthing and Mrs. Graham Copland. At present she was once more Ms. Stephanie Brayton.

So why not enjoy the invitation?

In the heavy mist he almost missed the movement on

the lawn in front of the Rhoadses' house. Plodding up the walkway was Cora Walton, her sturdy physique clothed in coat and muffler.

Without quite reasoning why, Maxim stepped on the brake and maneuvered the nearly noiseless car to the curb before Georgianna's house.

"I'll be just a minute," he assured his passenger as he opened his door and got out.

"Mrs. Walton!"

Cora rang Georgianna's bell before she turned to the summons. One couldn't be too careful, even in a quiet community. "Why, Mr. De Hoop!" she exclaimed in delighted surprise when the front-porch light revealed him. "Were you looking for me?" She peered out toward the front of her own house. "I didn't see you pull up."

"Actually, I was just driving by when I saw you on the walk," Maxim answered, sounding much more calm than he felt. Why the hell had he gotten out of the car to hail down a woman twice his age? Was he losing his mind? "I've been meaning to call . . . Why, hello, Mrs. Manchester."

"What are you doing here?" Georgianna barked ungraciously, glaring at the man on her steps.

"Hello, Georgianna." Cora glanced uncertainly at Maxim and then continued. "Mr. De Hoop saw me on the walk and wanted a word with me. I hope you don't mind if I invite him into your hallway for a moment. We're getting a bit damp."

"Come in, of course," Georgianna replied, embarrassed that Maxim's unexpected presence was making her forget her manners.

She didn't glance again at Maxim as he entered her hall, but it was unnecessary. In an instant she had taken in the expensive dark suit and knew that he was either going out or coming in from a fancy evening. He looked wonderful, healthy, virile, and exciting. There was probably a woman somewhere waiting for him. That thought, remarkably, did not cheer her.

"I only wanted to tell you about the response we've had to your new column, Mrs. Walton. Frank is delighted with the mail. After it ran in yesterday's paper, we even had a few calls." For the first time he turned to Georgianna. "I don't know if you're aware of it, but Cora's one of the *Chronicle*'s columnists."

"She knows it," Cora answered with a wink. "To give credit where credit is due, Georgianna's the one who should be praised for my column's new look. She even thought up the title."

Georgianna glanced away from Maxim's raised eyebrows. "Really, Cora, I only suggested a chattier approach to your style. You do the writing."

"Mutual admiration, I see."

Georgianna heard his slyly derisive tone and turned to face him squarely. "Cora and I happen to respect and admire one another, that's true. Respect is hard to come by these days, Mr. De Hoop."

"But surely not admiration," Maxim answered, his laser-bright eyes fully on her. She was still furious with him, as he'd expected. Suddenly an aroma prickled his nose, at once unusual and familiar. "Is that curry I smell?" he asked in disbelief.

"You see!" Cora said gleefully to Georgianna. "And you were worried that it wouldn't turn out properly."

"Smells don't tell the whole story," Georgianna cautioned. "The proof's in the tasting."

"I'm holding up your dinner," Maxim suggested.

"Yes," Georgianna replied before she could stop herself. Cora's blink of astonishment in the face of her rudeness made her backtrack quickly. "That is, Cora's consented to be a guinea pig for my first foray into Indian cooking. I'm teaching myself," she added with a defensive lift to her chin.

"She's quite good," Cora announced proudly. "Her young man will be delighted when he returns."

Maxim's amicable expression changed to brittle politeness. "Your husband likes curry? He's due home shortly?"

"Oh, no," Cora declared, forestalling Georgianna's reply in her enthusiasm for her young friend. "We'll have months to putter about in the yard and kitchen before he comes home. I've told Georgianna I'll make a thorough *hausfrau* out of her yet."

"And did you work before you were married, Mrs. Manchester?" he inquired.

"Yes," she snapped like the cracking of a whip.

Her chin was held in its delightfully stubborn way, yet just being in her presence made Maxim feel more lighthearted than he had in weeks. His smile deepened. As usual, her mere presence exhilarated him.

The opening of the storm door startled all three of the people in the hallway. "Please excuse me, but I was freezing out there."

Georgianna looked at the petite young woman who had stuck her head in the doorway. Georgianna nearly asked the woman how she could possibly feel the cold in the silver-blue fox coat she was wearing. But then she seemed so young, her piquant features nearly hidden by a thick mane of coppery hair, that it didn't seem right to insult her merely because she was Maxim De Hoop's ladyfriend.

Georgianna shot a look at Maxim, who was smiling openly. "Come in and introduce yourself, Stephanie. You will remember Mrs. Cora Walton."

Stephanie shook the hair out of her eyes with a practiced ease, then smiled at the older woman. "Mrs.? Oh! Of course, Mrs. Walton! How marvelous to see you." Without ceremony, she flung both arms about Cora's neck.

"Mrs. Walton taught Stephanie," Maxim said in an aside to Georgianna.

Georgianna didn't reply. She wasn't about to be drawn into friendly conversation with this man. All the same, she conceded reluctantly, she couldn't very well leave them all standing in her hallway. "Won't you come in and warm yourselves?" she asked, motioning toward the living room, where a fire blazed. "I just have to check something on the stove."

"Oh, we can't stay," Stephanie protested, "but I will at least introduce myself, since Maxim seems to have other things on his mind." She held out her hand. "I'm Stephanie Brayton."

"Georgianna Hel—Manchester," Georgianna answered, growing red-faced at her slip.

"Oh, do you have that trouble, too?" Stephanie questioned. "After my second divorce, I gave up trying to remember who I was. I decided to go back to my maiden name and leave it at that. The next man I marry gets to be the husband of Stephanie Brayton, period."

"How nice for him," Georgianna murmured, smiling maliciously at Maxim. "Excuse me. Please, Cora, all of you, do sit a moment."

"A short brandy would be nice," Georgianna heard Maxim say in reply to Cora's polite offer of refreshments.

"Hang the man!" she muttered as she opened the rice steamer. What was he up to now, bringing his girl friend into her home? Was he letting her know that he'd moved on to greener pastures?

"Some catch! 'After my second divorce . . . ,'" she mimicked.

"Caricature is seldom pleasant for the subject," a masculine voice said near her elbow.

Georgianna whipped around to face him, furious that he'd sneaked up on her. "You should know. Now kindly get out of my kitchen before I scald you."

Maxim couldn't believe how warm he felt. Just looking into her surprisingly dark eyes was like glimpsing a much sought after goal. "Georgie girl, all you have to do is look at me and I feel scalded," he said in an urgent but soft voice, and then turned and left.

The smile that had been in his eyes, the deeply felt tone of his voice, all of it combined to confuse and exasperate Georgianna as she scooped fluffy white rice into a warm casserole. He had no right to make her feel the way he did. He attracted her. It wasn't surprising. He was gorgeous, thoroughly masculine, and charming in a way she had never known a man to be. *She* had a right to be attracted. She was a free agent, unattached, single. But *he* believed that she was married.

That was what had bothered her from the beginning. He thought she was married and yet he didn't respect that fact.

Only once had he faltered in his obvious attempts to seduce her. And then it had taken precious little time for him to recoup from his surprise.

How could she like a man who didn't respect the most sacred vow that could be made between a man and a woman? He was the kind of man who would marry a dozen times, and never once be faithful. A playboy.

"Shall I ask them to stay for dinner?" Cora stood in the doorway this time, her expression uncertain. "I'm sorry, dear. I know you don't enjoy Maxim's company, and I had no idea he had a lady with him . . ." She made a helpless gesture with her hands. "We could wait a little before eating. Curry, I understand, only improves with age."

Georgianna shook her head. "There's enough to feed a maharajah's army. If it's edible, we might as well share."

And with that she followed Cora back into the living room.

With relief, she heard Maxim make his excuses and rise to his feet. "Another time?" he suggested in a hopeful tone.

"If Stephanie will agree to join us," Georgianna answered with a sugar-coated smile.

"Will you be coming to the *Chronicle* dinner dance?" Maxim asked Cora.

"I'll be there," Cora answered. "Georgianna hasn't

agreed to come, but I'm hoping to change her mind. I don't much care to drive after sundown.''

Frowning, Maxim looked from Cora to Georgianna and back. "I could send a car for you.''

"Oh, no!'' Cora disclaimed. "I'll be just fine. I haven't given up on my powers of persuasion yet. Georgianna says she hasn't a thing to wear." She glanced fondly at the subject of her conversation. "I told her she needn't worry, she'd look lovely in anything.''

"It's true,'' Stephanie chimed in, turning to Georgianna. "I was just thinking how lucky you are to have such lovely hair. I've spent enough money on mine to know that your color's natural. And what I wouldn't give for a few curves. Of course, I'm deathly afraid of hospitals, so cosmetic surgery is out of the question.''

Georgianna schooled her features to bland pleasantness in spite of her amazement at this frank speech. Without her coat, Stephanie was a mere wisp of a woman. But hers was an ethereal, Audrey Hepburn kind of beauty. Quite attractive. Beside her, Georgianna felt very sturdy and very tall. Only when Maxim came up to her did her sense of proportion reassert itself, for he topped her by several inches.

"Good evening, Mrs. Manchester, and thank you for your warm hospitality,'' he said, taking her hand and saluting in European fashion. "Don't forget, Cora, tomorrow night at six-thirty. I'll reserve a place for you at my table,'' he said as he bent and kissed the older woman's cheek.

When they were gone, Georgianna turned back to the kitchen.

"You will reconsider coming with me to the *Chroni-*

*cle*'s dinner dance won't you?'' Cora asked. ''I haven't been to a dance in years. I don't even know if my old standby gown will do. I must try it on in the morning. Of course, I'll understand if you prefer not to go.''

With a line like that, Georgianna had no choice. Surely there would be no harm in going, she thought, though she wasn't sure Alan Byrd would have agreed.

''I'd love to go, Cora. Honestly. Now, let's eat.''

Outside, as Maxim pulled away from the curb, Stephanie turned to him and said, ''I like her.''

''I agree. Cora Walton—''

''I meant Georgianna.''

Maxim's hand flexed on the steering wheel, but his tone didn't alter. ''I don't know what you're talking about, Steph. She's married.''

''In that case . . .'' Stephanie snuggled up closer. ''How about my place?''

He chuckled. ''We're old friends. I'd like it to stay that way.''

''Chicken?''

''Don't even think it.''

''Then I don't see the problem. I'm not asking for anything more than a little company tonight. You're lonely, I'm lonely. We might make history.''

He glanced at her upturned face and resisted the impulse to kiss her. ''What if you're disappointed?''

''Do you think I will be?''

''No.''

''Then where's the harm?'' She waited a moment before adding, ''We might find we're very comfortable together.''

Maxim's laughter was Sahara-dry. ''That's the trou-

ble. We'd be like a long-married couple going to bed and
doing what's natural." He shook his head. "Hardly an
exciting prospect."

Abandoning her attempts to unbutton his shirt, she sat
up and tossed her head in annoyance. "That's always
been your greatest fault, Max. You seem to think that
repeating a successful experience has got to be boring.
Married sex can be quite thrilling." With regal hauteur
she added, "I speak from vast experience."

His laughter was more easy this time. "Your experience doesn't say much for the married state, Steph.
What went wrong this time?"

"Oh, I don't think we were ever meant to get
married," she answered airily. "Graham and I should
have simply lived together." She heard him chuckle at
the irony of her words and hurried on. "The legal
complications of that marriage were incredible. Arrangements for the prenuptial agreements lasted longer
than the marriage. Oh, Max, let's not talk about that.
Graham was several kinds of a bastard, but he was good
in the sack."

"And just thinking about him has gotten to you," he
finished for her without a trace of rancor as he pulled into
her drive. "It's a good thing we've known each other so
long or I might be expected to pretend to be jealous. But,
as it is, I'm just not good company tonight."

Stephanie leaned over, covering his lips with an
openmouthed kiss. "You don't know what you're missing," she whispered when, at last, she drew away.

"I'm afraid I do now. Thanks. Go home, Steph," he
continued with a gentle push toward the door. "I'll pick

you up about six tomorrow night. Got to be there on time. It's expected of the guest of honor.''

She opened the door and then leaned back toward him once more. ''She must be something.''

''Who?''

''Cora Walton, of course,'' she answered sarcastically. ''Now don't get caught hanging about her block after curfew, Max. She might call the police. *Ciao!*''

Fifteen minutes later, when he had stopped in his own drive, Maxim didn't immediately get out of his car. While he hadn't wanted to admit it to himself, his reluctance to bed another woman was somehow locked up with his unquenchable desire for Georgianna Manchester.

A year ago he would never have looked back. But Georgianna's memory wouldn't let him go. It hung on, even after he thought he had banished her image by selling the photographs he'd taken that day to a national wire service. It was his policy to dismiss a subject from his mind once the sale had been made. His career had required a full-time commitment, no strings or considerations or responsibilities to keep a man from doing what he was paid to do. He was accustomed to moving on when a project was finished or useless.

Georgianna was a married woman. He didn't sleep with married women. That should have solved his problem—but it didn't. He still wanted her, as much as ever.

Maxim climbed out and stood in the frosty mist. Maybe she haunted him because he regretted hurting her. He had said harsh, brutal things, things he had never before said to any woman. The qualities that had attracted him to Georgianna had been her vulnerability and spirit. So why had he deliberately sought to bring her to her knees?

"I'm just getting soft in the head," he muttered. As the conflicting thoughts chased round in his head, he started toward his front door. There were no final conclusions to be drawn about his behavior toward the woman. But he knew, if given the chance, he'd like to share a quiet evening with Georgianna Manchester. Yes, he would like that very much.

# Chapter Eight

$\mathscr{G}$eorgianna leaned toward the mirror to check the new shade of mascara she'd recently purchased. Because her hair was a light golden shade of brown, cosmetic ladies automatically chose auburn or brown shades for her and were amazed at her insistence on charcoal or slate. But it was a fact, her lashes were nearly black.

She smiled at the dramatic change. The spiky sweep of lashes made her eyes the focus of her face, balancing the squared angles of her features. The brilliant shade of scarlet lipstick drew attention to the generous curves of her mouth. Most often she wore lipgloss, but she loved pulling out all stops when the occasion demanded it.

*Because he will be there.*

That thought didn't disturb her as much as it had the night before, she realized as she brushed through the hot-curled waves in her hair. With a twist of the brush, she flipped her bangs up and back. A few strands feathered her brow; the rest were swept back to one side.

The fact that he was seeing someone, especially someone as stunning as Stephanie Brayton, was proof that he'd given up pursuing her. Besides, the chance to spend an evening out tempered her reluctance to be in Maxim De Hoop's company. She wasn't even bothered by the fact that Maxim had called Cora and insisted on picking them up.

Georgianna reached for her dress and stepped into it, sliding the scarlet brocade fabric up over her smoky-colored hose and black tap pants. From the front the dress was a simple scarlet sheath. The back, however, made a daring plunge to the waist in a deep cowl.

It was an expensive dress, one that she had bought with her first paycheck and had not had an opportunity to wear before. But, she wondered as she looked at herself in the mirror, was it wise to wear it at a gathering of strangers? The full curves of her breasts pressing against the brocade fabric were quite provocative.

The doorbell sounded, interrupting her thoughts. After grabbing bag and jacket, she spritzed on a final spray of perfume, clipped on earrings of hammered gold, and hurried down the stairs.

"Coming!" she called, pausing in the hallway to slip on her coat. She didn't want Maxim offering to help her with it. For reasons she didn't pause to contemplate, she didn't ever again want to experience his touch.

"I'm ready," she declared when she opened the door.

"Yes, you are," he answered but there was a hint of

reserve in Maxim's voice as his eyes swept quickly over the tailored lines of her double-breasted black wool coat.

She spied a tuxedo tie beneath his black dress coat. "It didn't occur to me to ask if it was formal. Am I underdressed?"

Humor gleamed in Maxim's eyes as he considered a variety of provocative retorts to the opening she had provided. But he only said, "No, it's not formal. You look fine."

Georgianna's spirits faded. 'You look fine' was hardly reassuring. "Are you sure?"

"You look lovely, Mrs. Manchester. Shall we?"

Maxim reached out to take her by the elbow, but she turned away, avoiding that contact as she pretended to lock the door. *Don't touch me,* she thought. *Please don't touch.*

When she turned, he'd moved away. There was a puzzled look on his face, but he didn't try to touch her again as she descended the steps ahead of him.

She wasn't surprised to find a chauffeured limousine parked before the house. Somehow she'd known he would do the evening up in style. What she was surprised to find was Stephanie Brayton inside, tucked into one corner.

"Hello, Georgianna!" Swathed from head to knee in white fur, Stephanie indicated that Georgianna should slide onto the seat beside her. "Maxim won't mind sitting opposite us, will you?"

"Not when it gives me an uninterrupted view of two sexy women," he answered as he climbed in. "The next house, Tom," he said, motioning to the driver.

"You look so . . . different," Stephanie said admiringly. "Not that you didn't look pretty last night. But I had the impression that you were younger. Just how old are you?"

"Twenty-four," Georgianna responded, not at all embarrassed by the question.

"Why, you're just a baby compared to some of us present. Isn't that so, Max?" she replied with an arch look at him.

"Last time I checked we were the same age, Steph," he returned blandly.

Georgianna's gaze swung back to Stephanie with startled abruptness. Too late, she realized how it must look. "I—I just can't believe it," she said lamely. "You look my age."

"See there, Max?" Stephanie asked with a triumphant look. "I don't look a day over twenty-four."

Maxim reached for the handle of the car door. "On that note I think I'll retreat."

Georgianna watched as he neatly extricated himself from the limousine and started up Cora's front walk. He moved gracefully in formal clothes, a fact that surprised her, considering she had once made the observation that he seemed more at home in a pair of jeans.

"Yes, he is," Stephanie said, as though she had read Georgianna's thoughts.

Georgianna turned to her. "I beg your pardon?"

Stephanie nodded toward Maxim. "He's gorgeous. I can't think why I ever let him get away. We were young, it's true, and inexperienced, but I should have known better."

Georgianna looked down at the beaded evening bag in

her lap. What was Stephanie trying to tell her, that she and Maxim were once lovers? That wasn't hard to guess.

"He's hard to like sometimes. Max at eighteen was little different than he is today. Serious to a fault. And incurably restless. I think that's what frightened me off. He didn't see the need to flatter a girl with trivial compliments. Back then he had plans that included all the parts of the world I had no interest in. He always said he wanted to photograph front-page news, not print it. He's never had time to pursue a relationship until now."

Stephanie talked quietly but rapidly, as if sharing a confidence. "The responsibility of the De Hoop Publishing Corporation has him caged in at last. Thank God. But now he refuses to take time off."

Georgianna studiously smoothed the fold of her coat. She wasn't interested in Maxim's trials and tribulations.

"He's not an empire builder, that's true," Stephanie continued without missing a beat. "I doubt he'll stay tied to a desk beyond the end of the year. Over the last months he's been in every town where the family owns a paper. Once he's seen it all, he'll hire somebody to do the drudge work and he'll be off again. When he's ready to go, stopping Maxim is like trying to halt a bullet with a flyswatter."

"He does seem to be a man who does what he wants," Georgianna conceded softly.

That thought stayed with her on the drive to the Plowden Country Club. Seated across from him, she was keenly aware of his lazy perusal of her. Once, when he crossed his legs, his knee bumped hers. The jolt was like an electric charge, and she jumped.

Simultaneously they murmured, "Sorry," then she

glanced guiltily at Cora and Stephanie, who were engrossed in conversation.

"You look very nice tonight, Mrs. Manchester," Maxim ventured after a moment. When she merely smiled and turned to talk with the other women, he fell into silence.

Watching her in this uninterrupted way was a new experience for him. He hadn't seen her in repose since the day he'd photographed her. Now she was aware of him, as he was of her. Her every heartbeat echoed inside of him. Her nervousness betrayed itself in the slight trembling of her clasped fingers. Had they been alone he would have put his hands over them to smooth away that treasonous tremor. Incredible, yet the feeling persisted that she was afraid. Of him? *Impossible!*

Maxim turned suddenly to stare out into the night. She wasn't that special. He'd known many women more beautiful. Certainly her sophisticated makeup and hairstyle were attractive. That was their purpose, to attract. But he might have passed her on the street without another glance if not for . . .

No, that wasn't true. She hadn't deliberately brought herself to his attention. He'd been drawn to her when she had been windblown and salt-sprayed, totally unconscious of his presence. He'd wondered what it would be like to taste her sea-salted skin. He wondered now.

*She's married.*

That thought was usually an antidote to his musings, but not tonight. For the past two weeks he had convinced himself that he didn't want anything more to do with Georgianna Manchester. But watching her now, noting the defiant jut of her chin as his gaze lingered on her, he

wanted to know all there was to know about her. In spite
of her protest and the taboo of her marriage, they were
attracted. That fact alone was worth investigating.

"Will you tell your husband about this evening?" he
asked suddenly, his deep voice cutting smoothly across
the lighter chatter.

Georgianna didn't pretend to misunderstand him.
"Edward will be delighted to know I'm getting out a
little."

"Then we must give him more opportunities to be
pleased in the future." Maxim smiled slowly, ignoring
Stephanie's speculative gaze and Cora's concerned one.

A few minutes later, they were being ushered into the
country club's ballroom.

"Check your coat, ladies?" asked one of the young
girls behind the counter.

"Why, thank you, dear," Cora said as Maxim helped
her.

"Not on your life!" Stephanie declared gaily when he
turned to her. "I'm still shivering from the walk from
the curb. Oh, there's Frank. I'll bet he's looking for us.
Come on, Mrs. Walton, let's set his mind at rest.
Frank!" she called, steering Cora toward the ballroom.

"Your coat?"

Georgianna found herself looking straight into Maxim's china-blue eyes. "Your coat," he repeated.

Turning her back to him, she felt a sudden chill that
had nothing to do with the temperature of the night
outside. Slipping first one, then another button from its
hole, she told herself it was too late to regret her choice
of dress.

His fingertips, surprisingly warm, grazed either side

of her neck as he reached forward to lift the coat from her shoulders. The sensation of his touch remained as the garment was slipped down her arms. She heard his faint intake of breath with mingled delight and nervousness. And then she turned to face him.

His gaze moved over her, pausing on the swell of her breasts. His hands crushed the collar of her coat. When she'd answered her door, he had thought what he could see of her dress to be rather plain despite the bright color. How wrong he'd been.

The dramatic back plunge of the dress had revealed the exquisite line of her spine. Now that she faced him, he discovered the equally beautiful curves of her breasts. Yet, he couldn't think of anything to say to her. Certainly he couldn't say the things that came to mind.

"Is it appropriate?" she questioned, unnerved by his silent stare.

"It's fine," he assured her. But just thinking about watching her all evening in that slinky sheath, knowing that she was deliciously near-naked beneath its shimmery surface, was causing him very male discomfort. If she were free, he'd sweep her out of here in two seconds to someplace quiet, secluded, and alone.

As he accepted two tickets for the coats, he wondered cynically just how much more he could take before he gave up his recent pretense of simple curiosity about her. What he really wanted to know was what it would be like to have her naked in his arms, her body flushed and trembling with the fever of passion, warm and pliant, open for his . . .

He uttered a curse, refusing to finish his red-hot musings. It was going to be a long, long night.

Georgianna took his arm and followed him into the ballroom. In three-inch heels she was nearly his height, but that didn't take away from his magnetic presence one bit. Just walking at his side seemed to draw attention that she doubted she could have engendered on her own.

"Max! At last!" The man, blond and lean and in his mid-thirties, pumped Maxim's hand as he patted him on the back. "We've been waiting for you to begin, guest-of-honor." He paused, his eyes moving significantly between Maxim and Georgianna. "Don't tell me. This is the myster—"

"Frank, you're about to make a fool of yourself," Maxim cut in neatly. "This is Mrs. Edward Manchester. Georgianna, I'd like you to meet the *Chronicle*'s usually astute managing editor, Frank Howard."

"It's a pleasure to meet you," Georgianna said, extending her hand with a smile of sympathy for the embarrassed man.

"I should know better than to second-guess Max," Frank replied as he shook her hand. "At least some man has had the good sense to snatch you up. Is your husband with you?"

"He's at sea, serving his country," Maxim answered dryly. "Isn't that Beth Ryder at our table?"

Georgianna saw Frank glance perplexedly at Maxim's smiling face before he said, "As the guest of honor, you have a place on the dais, Max, with the mayor and his wife, and yours truly. Georgianna, of course, is invited to join the rest of the staff at one of the front tables."

"I hope you don't mind," Maxim murmured to Georgianna as they followed Frank through the labyrinth of tables filling half of the ballroom. "I had hoped we'd sit together. All of us," he added, belatedly realizing where his thoughts were carrying him. He'd wanted to have her to himself for a while and this night might be his only opportunity.

"I'll sit with Cora," Georgianna suggested. "And Stephanie makes good company."

"As long as you don't pay any attention to her," Maxim added under his breath. With a quick squeeze of her hand which left her fingertips throbbing in delight, he turned toward the long white-clothed table that had been set up on the stage.

As she watched, he stopped at every table along the way to speak personally to someone. The laughter and raised voices of welcome were genuine. He looked at home in the world, whatever he was doing. What she had labeled arrogance and conceit was, she conceded, a complete faith in himself. It drew people like the warmth of the sun.

Many of those present wore furs and expensive clothes and jewelry, the mark of wealth. Others in the crowd of several hundred were from more modest circumstances. From Stephanie's conversation in the car, she'd gleaned that Maxim had requested that everyone who worked for the *Chronicle*, including the janitor and the paperboys, be invited tonight. Yet she doubted the crowd's enthusiasm was engendered by his position as their employer. He possessed that marked but intangible essence called charisma.

When he finally made his way to the front and stepped up into the bright light, she was struck again by his unusual looks. There were other good-looking men present—Frank Howard was quite good-looking, for example—but none of them exuded that sheer power of attraction.

"Max should think of running for office," Stephanie remarked to Frank Howard as he stopped by their table between the first and second courses. "He looks absolutely delicious in the spotlight. I shudder every time I think about him thrashing around in some backwater country, risking his life for a few wretched pictures of even more wretched people. Pulitzer or no, he should've been doing something really significant."

"Like modeling or acting, perhaps?" Georgianna suggested innocently, gaining the laughter of those seated at the table.

"She's got you there, Steph," Frank teased. "We don't want Max dodging bullets in Lebanon or Central America, either. We want him right here in the driver's seat. He's a natural as a corporate executive. But maybe he can pursue photo journalism here, too. I understand his most recent sale came from a photo session taken in his own backyard."

"I saw the spread," Stephanie replied, her gaze switching to Georgianna. "I should be jealous."

Perplexed by the knowing look, Georgianna asked, "Jealous of his passion for photography?"

Stephanie and Frank exchanged glances.

"I wouldn't spoil it for the world," Frank murmured cryptically.

Stephanie shrugged and changed the subject. "Max doesn't know it yet, but I'm going to do him a world of good, take him away from all this printer's ink and corporate structure."

Frank grinned broadly. "Sorry, love. Max's remarks

tonight include an announcement of policy changes he plans to undertake next year. He didn't spend the past months learning the inner workings of his newspapers just to leave us high and dry. Hmm. Looks like my filet is getting cold," he observed as he turned toward the dais. "Save a dance for me, both of you."

Georgianna ate her meal in silence, content to listen to the talk of her table companions instead of the clang and wheeze of a basement furnace. Anything was better than being alone and waiting.

Midway through the main course she glanced toward the dais and met Maxim's gaze. She didn't know how long he had been watching her, but the impact of his stare was instantaneous.

Her stomach muscles tightened as her hand stopped its movement toward her mouth and lowered the forkful of food back to her plate. A slow throbbing began within her, at once familiar and frightening.

A touch on his arm diverted Maxim's attention, and he turned his head. Amazed by her sudden weakness, she sagged back against her chair as the delicious sensations rippling through her crested and then ebbed.

Utterly astonished, she stared unseeingly at her plate. What was happening to her?

"Ladies and gentlemen. If I may have your attention, please?"

She looked up at the sound of Frank's voice magnified by the loudspeaking system. Focusing her gaze on the tall, fair-haired man, she willed herself not to look again at Maxim. But his presence in her peripheral vision seemed to block out everything else, including Frank's introduction. Only when Maxim had moved to the microphone did she hear the applause of those about her and belatedly join in.

He dominated the podium as he did every other space he occupied, she thought. Under the white hot glare of the stage lighting, his features appeared even stronger than usual, projecting the confidence of a man completely at ease. She didn't listen to his words, they didn't really concern her, but the deep masculine cadence of his voice compelled her to watch him, deepening the confusion she felt. She hadn't mistaken his look. He wanted her. And she, what did she want?

After the mandatory quips and usual thanks, Maxim ended his short speech with, "I can't promise that you will like all the changes I have in mind. I'd be disappointed if you did. But I promise you, the future will bring differences. The *Plowden Chronicle* will be more than, as one of my subscribers recently put it, 'a series of grocery ads held together by leftover bits from newspaper wire services'!"

"Georgianna, are you all right?" Cora questioned as the younger woman choked.

Georgianna nodded, caught her breath, and erupted in laughter. Her throaty feminine chuckle turned several masculine heads in her direction but she was hardly aware of their admiration. Maxim De Hoop had quoted her in public. Once more applause swelled around her and she joined in.

"I have one request before the band gets underway," Frank said when he had replaced Maxim at the podium. "Will all members of the *Chronicle* staff please come up to the dais for a group picture? Quickly, please."

"I *love* to dance." Slipping off the jacket of her black

suit, Stephanie bared the backless halter. top she wore beneath. Sequined in iridescent bugle beads, it flashed and shimmered with every move she made as she undulated her shoulders to the rhythm of the drummer who was impatiently tapping out a beat. "Let's boogie!"

Georgianna wished momentarily that she'd come with her own date and could look forward to a night of dancing. She flashed a quick look at Maxim, posing with his employees, and then turned away. No, she didn't really hope he would ask her to dance. She was frightened of his effortless power to move her. Locked in his embrace, moving to the suggestive rhythm of a slow dance, lord, it would be like touching fire to ice. She would melt at his feet!

"Dance, Georgianna?"

She looked up a few minutes later to see Frank standing over her, his hand extended.

"Oh yes, do, dear," Cora encouraged. "Frank wasn't one of my best pupils but he certainly was one of the best dancers Plowden High School ever graduated."

Georgianna smiled, but shook her head. "Thank you, Frank, but I'd better not. My pulse says yes, but my back says no."

Frank waited, as if expecting her to continue with her explanation. When she didn't, he smiled a little stiffly and turned to the other woman. "Cora, would you like to dance with one of P.H.S.'s finest?"

"Thought you would never ask," Cora responded, rising quickly to her feet. After a last thoughtful glance at Georgianna, she left the table.

After they had gone, Georgianna closed her eyes and propped her chin on her hand. Subterfuge and lying were not her best suit. Cora had seen right through the flimsy excuse. But that was just too bad. She couldn't very well dance with some men and then refuse to dance with her host. She didn't want to see Stephanie in Maxim's arms, nor did she look forward to the moment when he would ask her to dance and she would have to embarrass herself and anger him.

She sighed deeply. She felt like an emotional yo-yo. Every other moment she wished she hadn't come.

To her mingled relief and pique, Maxim did not approach her table in the first hour. While she turned down invitation after invitation, she saw his dark head appear in the crowd of dancers at regular intervals, each time with a different partner. As for Stephanie, she never once left the dance floor.

When the band paused for a fifteen-minute break, she saw Maxim guiding Stephanie toward her table. Instinct took over. Grabbing up her purse, she murmured "Excuse me" to her companions and headed for the ladies' room. The truth was, she admitted to herself as she angled away from the pair, she wanted very badly to dance with Maxim and she didn't trust herself to refuse if he asked her.

*Hiding out in the rest room is a high school antic*, she chided herself as she whiled away the minutes adjusting her makeup and combing her hair. If she'd had any real fortitude she never would have come. Perhaps she should just make her excuses and ask someone to call a cab for her.

*Maxim wouldn't allow that.*

Of course, he'd insist on seeing her home. Sitting beside him in the back seat of a limousine would be nearly as bad as dancing with him. If he insisted, it would disrupt the party which was in his honor. No, there was nothing for her to do but brave out the next few hours.

The sound of music came as a relief. The one saving grace about retiring to the rest room was that no one would ask her what she had been doing, she decided as her humor reasserted itself. With a determined look on her face, she pushed the door open and stepped out.

"At last."

She jumped as a firm hand grasped her by the upper arm. She swung around to confront Maxim, who'd obviously been waiting for her.

"Sorry I startled you," he said, a frown drawing his dark brows together. "Are you feeling okay? Frank said something about your back bothering you."

She smiled brightly. This was her out. "I made the mistake of wearing my favorite pair of heels. They're murder on my back."

For emphasis, she lifted her foot to display a skimpy sandal with an ankle strap and spiky heel.

His brows arched wickedly and his smile returned as he fastened an interested gaze on the slim leg in sheer black hose. Belatedly she realized he might misinterpret her gesture as a come-on.

"I've a remedy for that," he announced and, to her utter astonishment, dropped to one knee. "Give me your foot," he demanded, smiling up at her.

She darted quick embarrassed looks about them, whispering, "Get up, you'll dirty your pants-leg."

Amusement glittered in his amazingly blue eyes. "Give me your foot, Georgie," he coaxed.

They were blocking the door to the ladies' room, yet Georgianna had the feeling that he was going to kneel there until she gave in. With a murmured "You nut!" she raised her foot.

He took her ankle in a warm caressing grip and braced her shoe against his knee so that he could unfasten the tiny buckle with his free hand. Unwillingly, Georgianna placed a hand on his shoulder to keep her balance.

She didn't have the nerve to watch him. Instead, she stared out over the heads of the few people in the hallway. But she couldn't block out the sensation of his touch, at once light and incredibly intimate. His fingers encircled her ankle, his thumb rubbing an erotic massage into her very bones. "Hurry up!" she whispered raggedly, her fingers curling into the soft fabric of his coat.

"Why should I, when the view is so spectacular?" he murmured.

Meeting his superheated gaze was a mistake. A fury of blood swept her face, stinging her cheeks to cherry red. From his angle below her, with her hem hiked over her knees, he must be able to see a great deal.

"The other foot," he said softly, his eyes never moving from her face.

When she switched, she was better able to keep her balance in her bare foot and released her grip on his shoulder. But she had been ignited by that one scorching look, and she no longer wanted to pretend that she was not as attracted as he.

It was the most natural thing in the world to take his arm and follow him out onto the dark, crowded dance floor when he rose with her shoes in his hand. She didn't resist, or protest that she was barefoot. She didn't mention her back or propriety or even that she'd be insulting the many men who'd already asked her. She went into Maxim De Hoop's arms with one thought: she had hoped for and feared this moment from the instant she had agreed to attend the dance.

The music had a slow tempo but, once in his arms, she knew it wouldn't have mattered even if it were fast-paced. They moved to their own slow rhythm of desire.

Fingers threaded through hers, he let her shoes dangle by the straps from the crook of his little finger. His free hand pressed possessively against her back, the finger-tips curving into the plunging neckline and resting against the indentation of her naked spine.

A ripple of sheer joy radiated outward from that touch, the merest pressure of those fingers redoubling her pleasure as he guided her about the floor.

He didn't speak, but there was no need. The insistent brush of his thighs against her legs promised a passion she had never known. The slight abrasion of his dinner jacket against the unrestricted lushness of her breasts was a sweet agony from which she wished no relief.

Every move he made, every step, brought her closer against him until they were no longer really dancing at all. He held her breathlessly tight. After a few minutes he stepped back on one foot, pulling her against him, and neatly parted her knees with one of his. His hips flowed against hers, teasing, demanding a response to his blatantly erotic play.

She was melting inside, drowning in her own desire for him. There was an urgency beneath his languid passion that she hadn't experienced with him before, not even when he'd kissed her.

Her hand curled on his neck, feeling the rapid but solid rhythm of his pulse under her thumb. *He knows how affected I am by our dancing,* she thought.

Yet when she tilted her head to look up at him, there was no triumphant grin on his face. The broad planes were hard and tense, the angle of his nose sharper than usual. The sensual mouth was a hard line of self-restraint. And yet there was no denying that need. Beneath her hand the muscles of his neck were rigid. His hips no longer melted into hers but had grown taut with a need that demanded privacy.

As he bent toward her, she turned her head away, afraid that he would kiss her here in front of people to whom she'd just been introduced as a married woman.

Instead, he placed his smooth-shaven cheek against hers, his lips nearly touching her ear. "Let's get out of here. Now!"

"The others?" she whispered huskily, hardly able to create any sound.

"To hell with the others! This is between you and me." His tone was clipped, but he trembled slightly beneath her hands, and the knowledge that he was as vulnerable as she to the passion between them encouraged her.

It wasn't really wrong, after all, she reasoned through the tidal push and pull of her own reluctance. As soon as they were alone, she'd tell him that she wasn't really married. She'd tell him that she was divorced or widowed, something that would provide an excuse until she was able to tell him the truth. For she could no longer bear to keep up the pretense that she didn't want him, that she loved someone else.

The music stopped. For a long moment Georgianna was catapulted beyond her senses, continuing to move to an inner melody of her own. Maxim didn't release her. If anything, he seemed to draw her in even tighter, as though he could absorb her through his clothes. "Now!" he repeated in an urgent whisper.

"Smile!" came the cheerful demand an instant before a blue-white flash exploded in their faces.

Georgianna cringed, throwing her hand up instinctively as a second flashbulb illuminated the darkened room.

"Stop!" she cried, twisting in Maxim's arms to hide her head against his shoulder.

"What the hell do you think you're doing!" Maxim demanded in an angry hiss. He lunged at the photographer and grabbed the camera out of the stunned young man's hands.

"I—I'm Larry Bostick, Mr. De Hoop, photographer for the *Chronicle*," the man answered. "Mr. Howard told me to get some informal shots of the party for the society page of Sunday's paper. You made such a striking couple, I . . . I . . ." His voice trailed off as the lights came on.

"Taking pictures for publication without permission is against the law," Georgianna protested, rapidly regaining control of herself. "You can't print that shot, I won't let you!"

Maxim heard her protest in surprise. He'd assumed she was merely unpleasantly surprised by the flash, but when he turned to her, several new reasons for her distressed expression came to mind. They'd been locked in an embrace, dancing or no. It didn't take a photographer's imagination to guess how that shot would look in the papers.

Without a moment's hesitation, he flipped open the camera and extracted the half-exposed roll of film. "Sorry, Larry, the lady's right. No," he said, forestalling protest. "Since you're my employee, this roll of film belongs to me. What I do with it is my business." He turned to Georgianna and held out the roll. "I apologize."

Georgianna took it, closing her fingers tightly over it. "Thank you," she said with more emotion than the incident demanded. He couldn't know what it meant to her, but he'd just saved her from grave danger. No publicity of any kind, Alan had warned her. If she were being hunted, the newspapers would be one of the sources sure to be watched.

"All right, the excitement's over. Back to the original entertainment," Maxim directed with a signal to the band. Immediately they began playing a hard-rocking tempo which delighted the younger members of the crowd. Before he could turn back to Georgianna, the lights dimmed.

"Are you okay?" he questioned as he slipped an arm about her waist.

"Sorry," she murmured. "I feel ten kinds of a fool for making such a scene. Let's go sit down, please."

"You had every right to be angry," he answered tightly, his own anger at the photographer fueled by a different source.

Georgianna had been about to capitulate; he had felt her melting in his arms. Another moment and they'd have been out of here. Now they were on the spot, everyone had seen them together, and she couldn't walk out with him. He didn't blame her. It was his fault for pressing her when the time wasn't right. But at least he knew now that she did want him. Nothing would stop them next time.

He ignored a twinge of conscience. He didn't believe for a minute that she was deliriously happy, married to her sailor. If she had been, he couldn't have gotten to her. If she were his wife, he wouldn't have gone off and left her. He would have so entwined her life with his that she'd never have time to look at another man.

"So there you are, Georgianna. We had about decided that you'd disappeared," Stephanie volunteered when they reached the table. "Max, you had no right to frighten that young man like that. He probably thinks he's lost his job."

"He should," Maxim snapped with a cold look at Frank. "Don't you teach your staff manners?"

Frank shrugged, not at all offended. "Did you take yours to Beirut last year?"

Maxim made an ominous sound, but said nothing as he pulled out Georgianna's chair, then went around and seated himself in a vacant chair on the other side of Stephanie.

Georgianna met every set of eyes at the table expectantly, but no one else made any mention of the incident.

For the next hour she directed all her conversation to Cora. If Cora seemed a little cool, it didn't stop her from lending Georgianna her sympathetic support.

"I suppose I made a fool of myself," Georgianna

whispered much later, when the rest of those at the table had gotten up for the final dance.

Cora's gray eyes seemed to penetrate the younger woman. "For all it may seem, I don't often meddle in other people's business, Georgianna. But, because I like you very much, I'll say my piece. Maxim De Hoop is a fine young man. I'm proud to know him, to know his family. But he's a different breed. He's accustomed to getting what he wants. There's a ruthless streak in him, or he wouldn't have gotten as far as he has as quickly."

Georgianna waited for Cora to go on in that vein, but the older woman simply reached out and patted her folded hands. "My mother would say you've a gorgeous attraction for the devil here. Keep them busy, dear."

*Idle hands are the devil's workshop.* Aunt Mary's favorite phrase. "I'm thinking of taking up crocheting," Georgianna allowed with a wry smile.

Cora chuckled. "Can't help you there. My mother despaired of turning these hands to needlework before I was ten. That's why I took up the trowel. It's been love ever since."

The ride home was accomplished in near-silence, with Stephanie whispering now and again to Maxim. Georgianna was surprised to realize she didn't care. It was as though nothing anyone could say or do could alter in any manner the accord between Maxim and herself. She had no idea what the result of that accord would be. The inner music hummed inside her still, even after the mood-shattering episode on the dance floor, even after Cora's commonsense lecture, even after she'd decided not to let him in tonight.

"I'll be just a minute," Maxim told Stephanie as he helped Georgianna out of the limousine.

They had let Cora out first, and Maxim had escorted her to her door. As Georgianna looked across the lawn, she half-expected to see Cora watching them from her living room window. She was surprised—and relieved—to see the upstairs bedroom light go on. Cora trusted her.

Maxim took the key she offered him, looking into her face for the first time since they'd left the dance floor.

"I want to come back," he said softly, pretending to search for the key.

"No."

Maxim frowned. "Georgie, I—"

She almost shook her head, then remembered that Stephanie would be watching them. "Not tonight."

Maxim stared at her. She hadn't said no. She'd said "not tonight."

"I'll call you," he promised as he turned the key in the lock. Reaching inside the door, he flipped on the hallway light.

Nothing happened.

"Light's burned out," he commented as he pushed the door open to allow her to enter.

But Georgianna didn't move. Suddenly she realized that the porch light was not on either. She knew she had turned it on before she left. "Are you certain you flipped the right switch?"

He reached in and flipped two different switches. "Porch and front-hall lights are both out. You must have blown a fuse. Do you want me to take a look?"

Georgianna backed up a step from the yawning dark beyond the doorway. "No," she whispered hoarsely.

Fingers of dread circled her heart. She'd left the hall light on as well as the porch light. She'd done it because she didn't want to enter a dark house.

Why would the fuse blow?

Maybe it hadn't. Maybe someone had fixed it so that she would enter a dark hallway when she returned. Maybe someone was waiting for her.

Georgianna began to tremble. "I . . . I don't want . . . I can't go in there!"

# Chapter Nine

$\mathcal{D}$on't tell me you're afraid of the dark?" Maxim chided gently. "Come on, I'm more than a match for a blown fuse."

Georgianna jerked her arm free of his grasp as he tried to pull her toward the door. "No! I mean, I . . . I . . ."

Frantic, she searched for words that would make sense of her nameless terror. If she shouldn't go in there, neither should he.

"Maybe there're burglars," she said weakly.

His derisive laughter would have angered her at any other time. Now she heard it only as a sign of his determination to enter the Rhoadses' house. "All right, scaredy-cat. You can wait in the car while I tour the first floor. Look, there's a light on in the kitchen. Thieves wouldn't cut one line and not the others."

No, Georgianna conceded. Thieves wouldn't. But an

assailant hiding in the dark to catch her unaware wouldn't need much of a distraction. The time she would spend frowning at the light switch would be enough.

"Let's call the police." She gripped his coatsleeve as he started inside. "Please. It might be someone . . . some kind of . . ." His disbelieving gaze halted her stammering.

"Have you reason to suspect something, Georgianna?" Maxim turned to face her fully for the first time. She was quaking. He felt the tremors running through her hand on his sleeve.

"I just don't want to go in," she admitted. Yet even as she said it, she was beginning to imagine the stir it would cause in the neighborhood if she called the police. They might come with sirens and lights. They'd light up the house and search the grounds. They'd expect explanations. No, she mustn't call the police either.

"I'm going in," Maxim said when his impatience overcame her reluctance to speak. "Go back to the car and tell Stephanie I'll only be a minute."

Georgianna shook her head, her fingers sliding down his arm to grasp his hand. "No, I'll go in, too. I'm being silly, I know it. Only . . ."

"Only it's not even your house and you aren't quite comfortable here on a good night," Maxim finished for her with a sympathetic smile. "I know. I've been in that very situation more times than I like to remember. You don't have to come in yet."

Gaining confidence from his matter-of-fact tone, Georgianna smiled faintly. "I'll go." If there were danger, it was there because of her and he should not face it alone.

She started in the door first, but he halted her. "Wait." He turned and hurried down the walkway to the car. A few seconds later he came running back, a flashlight in his hand. "I'm brave but not stupid," he teased as he flicked the switch and a beam of light lit up the hall. "Give me your hand, and stay behind me."

Georgianna slipped her cold hand into his warm one and bravely stepped inside.

It didn't take long to traverse the hall and reach the living room. "Right wall," she instructed as he felt for the light switch. Nothing happened.

"That doesn't surprise me," Maxim said, speaking his thoughts aloud for her benefit. "Houses are wired in series. If the fuse blows, all the lights on that circuit go out. We'd do better to try a light in the rear or on another floor."

"The kitchen light's on," she reminded him. "Maybe you're right."

Maxim gave her hand a tight squeeze and she moved up against him until she was hugging his back with her body. He didn't comment, because her hand was as cold as ice.

In the hallway leading back to the kitchen, they found the first light that worked.

"My guess is that the front hallway, living room, and possibly the dining room are wired to the same fuse," Maxim said when the bathroom light came on. "Sometimes, though, you'll find lights on opposite sides of the house wired in together." He smiled at her. "Scared you, didn't it? Poor thing," he murmured, holding her against his chest.

Georgianna went willingly, laying her head on his

shoulder. Even so, she couldn't stop the nagging doubt that upstairs, or even in the basement, an intruder might wait. The house was huge. A man could hide . . .

"Hey, what's this?" Maxim questioned as she began violently shaking. He caught her chin in one hand and tenderly smoothed back the hair from her face with the other. "Still unconvinced? Would you like to spend the night somewhere else? We can always come back in the morning to switch the fuses."

Georgianna saw desire stir once again in his eyes. If she agreed to go somewhere with him, to his home or a hotel, he would make love to her.

"I can't desert my job," she whispered desperately, already drowning in the flood of emotions roused once too often this night. "I was hired to protect this house."

"Then I'll come back with you," he said, and leaned forward to quickly kiss her mouth. "You're icy cold, Georgie, but I'll fix that shortly."

She didn't resist as he pulled her back through the front hall and out the door. When he'd locked the door, he led her down the steps to the car.

"Georgianna's blown a fuse," he explained as he climbed in and handed the chauffeur the flashlight.

Stephanie regarded the two of them in surprise. "I don't understand. Why didn't you exchange it for a new one, Max?"

"She's out of fuses," Maxim answered smoothly as he closed the door after himself. "Take Ms. Brayton home first, Tom. Then we'll drive back toward town. There's bound to be some place open even at this hour of the night."

"Isn't that a bit drastic?" Stephanie asked, glancing

suspiciously from one to the other. "Georgianna has some light. I saw them go on at the back of the house while I sat out here damn near freezing to death. Couldn't this wait until the light of day?"

Maxim didn't bother to answer, and Georgianna couldn't think of anything to say that wouldn't make matters worse.

By the time they reached Stephanie's door, she was seething. "Don't bother, Sir Lancelot," she sneered, slamming the door practically on his foot. "I can look after myself!"

"I'm sorry," Georgianna murmured when Stephanie had disappeared inside her house and they had pulled away from the curb. "I spoiled your evening."

Maxim leaned forward to tap the driver on the shoulder. "Take us home, Tom. Barnes will have extra fuses, I'm certain."

Ignoring Georgianna's sound of protest, he said to her, "Are you always so afraid of the dark?" His tone was light but his expression was serious.

"I'm not the hysterical type, if that's what you mean," she answered defensively.

"That wasn't my impression either," he agreed. "No, I'd say you're the kind of person who'd have a good reason for expecting trouble. Is there a good reason, Georgie?"

"Why do you call me that?" she asked. He'd been shortening her name that way all evening without permission.

"Don't try to change the subject." His voice was a shade more harsh. "You must have some reason for expecting trouble. What is it, Mrs. Manchester?"

Georgianna bristled at the interrogation. She'd nearly forgotten that he was a newspaper man. His curiosity would urge him on when other people would realize that their questions had become an invasion of privacy.

"I didn't ask for your help." She gripped the purse in her lap a little tighter. "I was spooked by the unexpectedness of the situation." A vision of Stephanie's sneering face came to mind, and she thought fleetingly that the woman should never grimace. It gave away her age. "What more do you want? I apologized for spoiling your plans for the rest of the evening."

"What plans were those?" he asked pleasantly.

The volatile energy of her fear was redirected into anger. "Don't play games with me!"

His eyes traveled leisurely over her. "You're trembling again. Still afraid?"

"I'm furious!" Georgianna amended.

He nodded. "Transference of anger. It's more heartening to strike at a reality rather than to face the unknown. Go right ahead. I'm a substantial target."

"And don't patronize me!" she muttered miserably. Slowly the numbing fear that had tripped up her reason was receding and in its wake were the hundred unanswerable questions he'd be certain to ask. "I'm tired. I have a headache. Just take me home."

"Back to the house? What if another fuse blows? What if you were right, that someone is hiding somewhere? We didn't search upstairs or even check the basement. Do you really want to simply go back?" His voice was soft, almost soothing in quality. But his words were like tiny needles edging painfully under her skin.

The fear came back, sweeping through her until a faint moan escaped her.

Maxim crossed the space between them and pulled her into his arms in one smooth movement. "Oh, Georgie girl, don't. Don't."

She melted against him. It was like coming home to touch him, to feel his strength and heat offered as a protection against her own imagination. Even so, a part of her knew what he'd done and was indignant. "You don't play fair," she murmured.

"Not when the alternative is losing something I want very badly," he agreed quietly.

She had started backing away from him again, and he knew she'd leave him at her front door if he didn't stop her. He'd frightened her to make her admit that she needed him, but he hadn't meant to so demoralize her. Something was wrong, something she would not or could not confide in him.

"Don't you trust me, Georgie?"

"It isn't that," she said, belatedly remembering that they weren't alone. "I haven't been sleeping well, by myself, in a strange house. My husband would be amused," she added for the chauffeur's benefit.

"Then he's a damned fool!" Maxim didn't apologize for the words. Any man who would laugh at another person's misery deserves contempt.

Beside him Georgianna's mind was racing. Indecision. Each time Edward came up in conversation she was trapped by her inability to create any real enthusiasm for her phantom husband. She should defend him, but she didn't want to, not to Maxim De Hoop. She simply lay in his arms, her head resting in the curve of his neck and shoulder.

After a moment she placed a hand on his chest. There was no real reason for the action, but the solid, slow thud of his heart under her palm compelled her to leave it there.

The turn off the avenue would have been missed at night by a stranger. The wild tangle of berry vines and stark leafless branches all but obscured the narrow gravel road.

Georgianna sat up. "You live in the woods."

"Hardly." Maxim pointed out the window. "You'll see the house when we round the next curve."

Fifty yards down the track the road suddenly widened into a two-lane blacktop road. Seconds later the dark outline of an estate house came into view.

"The De Hoop monstrosity," he commented dryly. "Great-grandfather Willem is responsible for the disfiguring of the original Dutch Colonial design. His contributions were the wings on either side."

"I didn't realize just how wealthy you are," Georgianna said softly as the grand proportions of the house came into view.

Maxim knew she was remembering his sarcastic comment about the Rhoadses' house when he thought she owned it. "It's a roof over my head," he quipped. "Come on. You can wait inside."

After helping her out, he leaned back inside to speak to the driver.

The front door opened as they reached the top step, disconcerting Georgianna with the knowledge that someone had been watching them.

"This is Barnes, Georgianna;" Maxim said when he had ushered her into the foyer. "Barnes, meet Mrs. Manchester."

"How do you do?" Barnes replied without any expression in his tone.

"Hello, Barnes," Georgianna said, uncertain of what one was supposed to say to a butler. "It's awfully cold out."

The slight nod of his silver-white head was not reassuring. "Coffee and brandy in the library, Mister De Hoop?"

Maxim saw the guarded look Georgianna shot him. "Not this time, Barnes," he answered with a smile. "Mrs. Manchester's needs are out of the ordinary. Do we happen to have an extra fuse or two lying about?"

This time Barnes' granite face moved, the white brows winging upward. "A fuse, sir?"

"Electrical fuses, Barnes. Mrs. Manchester has blown a fuse. I thought you might be able to help us."

"Of course." With one speculative look at the lady in the black wool coat, a very good sign of taste in his opinion, Barnes bowed slightly at the waist. "There's a fire laid in the salon. Perhaps the lady would like to warm herself?"

A minute later, Georgianna stood in the salon with her hands raised to the roaring fire. Marble mantelpieces, Queen Anne antiques which even her inexperienced eye could recognize, and paintings and Turkish carpets— Maxim De Hoop was not only wealthy, he was a part of an empire.

"Like it?"

He'd come up to stand right behind her, his presence

more warming than any fire. One backward step and she could lean against him; she resisted the nearly overwhelming impulse. What had he asked her? "Yes, it's very impressive."

"You hate it."

Georgianna spun around to face him. "I didn't say that."

His gaze fastened on her mouth. "Say anything, Georgie. I like to watch your lips form words."

He didn't touch her, but he placed a hand on the mantel behind her, moving closer until she could feel his breath on her face. "Do you know that you pout when you speak? Especially when you say 'please' or 'don't.' Then there's the husky purr that tantalizes me every time you say my name. Say it, Georgie. Make me want to kiss you."

"Will these do, sir?"

The sound of Barnes' voice was a lifeline. Georgianna's lashes fluttered downward over her eyes, veiling the desire she knew Maxim could see there.

Maxim reacted without a trace of embarrassment. "Bring them here, Barnes," he said as he forced himself away from her and turned to the man. "These will do," he pronounced when he held them in his hand. "Did Tom bring my car around?"

"Yes, sir." Barnes cast a last look at the lady, surprising a grateful expression on her face. Perhaps she hadn't sought Maxim's advances after all. He smiled. "Good evening, Mrs. Manchester. I hope I've been of help."

"You have," Georgianna responded. More help than he would ever know.

The Lamborghini purred as they swung out of the drive and back down the private road, but Georgianna could hardly appreciate the smell of the expensive leather upholstery and the soft sheen of the teakwood dashboard.

*Maxim De Hoop was a millionaire.*

For the first time she really understood what that meant. Not just extra money for little luxuries like this sleek foreign sportscar or full-length mink coats, he had command of wealth that included Van Vleck paintings and the services of a butler and chauffeur. He and she had nothing in common but desire and she wasn't even free to express hers under present circumstances.

A hand curled possessively over the top of hers. "I can hear you thinking from here," he said softly.

"Can you?" she challenged, positive that he couldn't possibly guess her thoughts.

"You're wondering if you should let me stay once we've solved your electrical problem."

Georgianna carefully kept her face in profile to him. "And what did I decide?"

"You haven't," he answered promptly.

The silence that fell between them lasted until they pulled up before the Rhoadses' house.

Gazing at the dark front of the house, Georgianna stiffened. "Did you turn on the upstairs lamp?"

"You know we didn't go upstairs," he answered as he set the handbreak. "You're not going to . . . Georgianna?"

She had covered her face with her hands and was slowly shaking her head.

"Damn!" he muttered, and grabbed her hands to jerk them away from her face. "Look at me!" he demanded. "Dammit, Georgianna! Is there something I don't know?"

She opened her eyes. She mustn't put him in danger. She mustn't! She would go inside alone and use the phone. She would call Alan and . . . and . . .

"It's Edward, isn't it?"

She looked up at Maxim in amazement. "What?"

"You're not happily married. You ran away from him, didn't you? He's looking for you and you're afraid he's found you, isn't that it?"

She didn't mean to laugh in his face, not when he was filled with worry and anxiety over her, but she could no longer control her emotional responses. The melodramatic turn of his imaginings struck her as hysterically funny.

Through her tears of mirth she saw his face alter into a mask of rage and she thought he would strike her. That was what people did when someone was hysterical.

The impact of his mouth on hers had the same stunning effect. It was not a lover's kiss; it demanded a surrender of another sort. Georgianna locked her arms about his neck, fusing their mouths together in a long hungry exploration.

Maxim broke away first, but he didn't release her. In the dark interior of the car her eyes shone with tears. "You won't trust me," he said after a moment.

She heard the hurt in his voice, but there was nothing to say. She couldn't trust him. In spite of their physical attraction she didn't know him very well. But she did know he could be ruthless in his dealings with people. She had witnessed that in his high-handed tactics with the photographer. He hadn't bothered to smooth over the awkward moment. Neither had he pulled any punches when she'd tried to fob him off a short while ago. If he decided her story would be the perfect scoop for his papers, he might use it.

Maxim patiently watched the changing pattern of expressions on her shadowed face. She was struggling with her need to trust him. He saw the decision with disappointment. Her chin angled outward. She wouldn't tell him. Yet.

"Come on, we're both tired," he said gently as he reached across her and opened the door.

On the steps Georgianna didn't say anything as he held out his hand for the door key. When he turned the key and the door opened she didn't even flinch. She'd done all she could do to warn him off.

A flashlight appeared in his hand, its beam of light marking a path through the dark hallway. "Where's the entry to the basement?" he asked as they walked through.

"In the hall behind the front stairwell," she answered. "But you needn't go down there. I can call a repairman. There're emergency numbers on the pad in the kitchen."

He turned to her, his face a Halloween mask of light and shadow. "Isn't it a bit late to be thinking of that?"

Of course he was angry. Who wouldn't be after the way she had behaved? "I'm sorry," she whispered.

"Hell!" He moved ahead, not waiting for her.

She'd forgotten about the chair jammed under the

basement doorknob. "Extra protection," she murmured weakly as he raised his brows.

"Maybe you should find another, less stressful occupation," he muttered as he unwedged the door.

The basement light came on instantly, to Georgianna's relief.

"A blown fuse," he said under his breath.

She didn't wait for him to invite her downstairs. Nothing would have kept her standing in the dark hall.

He looked about the finished rooms of the basement, which included a game room, office, and workroom. "Let's try the laundry room," he suggested.

The fuse box was in the wall opposite the washing machine, but Georgianna had never given it any thought. He flipped open the cover and ran his finger along the line of fuses until he found one that had burned out. Over his shoulder she saw his finger move to a neatly typed strip beside it. It read 'FRONT PORCH LIGHT, FRONT HALL, AND LIVING ROOM.' Without comment, he unscrewed the bad fuse, fished the new ones out of his pocket to compare them, chose the right size, and replaced it.

"All done," he said less than a minute after opening the box.

"I feel like a fool." Georgianna shook her head. She had gone off half-cocked. It was her greatest failing. With just a little thought, she wouldn't have panicked so completely.

"It's been a hell of a night," he murmured, his own frustration easing. He embraced her shoulders with an arm. "Let's go back upstairs and check everything out."

She made no comment when he replaced the chair under the doorknob after relocking the door. ''I'll follow you,'' he said.

The hallway light was on now, as was the front-porch light. The living-room lights came on at the touch of a switch. Aware of his tread behind her, she went from room to room on the first floor. Everything was just as she had left it. When she finished the tour, they were back in the front hall.

''What about upstairs?''

Georgianna looked up the stairway, undecided as to whether he was teasing her or not. ''Unnecessary,'' she answered after a short pause.

He didn't even curse this time, just took the steps two at a time. She followed.

He was very thorough. In each of the three bedrooms on the right side of the hall, he opened each closet and looked under each bed. At first she wanted to stop him, to protest that he was making her feel more foolish with each action. But there was something in his expression that silenced her. He was protecting her, assuring her that she was safe because he'd made her so.

That thought brought the sting of tears to the back of her eyes, but she knew she wouldn't shed them. He cared. He cared about her a great deal. And that in itself made her feel safer.

Her bedroom was last. He paused before entering it, as if he needed her permission.

She stepped in ahead of him, her eyes skimming quickly over the chairs and bed, hoping she'd put away her clothes.

When she turned back to him, he was still standing in the doorway.

"Well, I guess that's it," she said nervously.

"I haven't checked your closet . . . or your bed," he answered quietly.

There was nothing quiet about his gaze. She'd slipped out of her coat in the living room and she saw his delft-blue eyes brighten as they swept over her.

"Come here, Georgie."

She never knew whether he said it aloud or only thought it, but Georgianna moved across the floor and into his arms with no hesitation.

She needed no arousing; he'd done that hours earlier on the dance floor. Now she needed to be fulfilled.

All the fear and doubt she'd experienced in the last weeks fled until there was only the sensual delight of his embrace. As his lips found hers and parted them, seeking to explore the erotic cavern of her mouth, a whimper of assent issued softly from Georgianna. She thrust both hands through his thick dark hair, fingers cradling his head as she swayed against him.

With a hand at her waist, Maxim guided her sideways until his back met the solid barrier of the bedroom wall. Then his free hand joined the first, in a slow heavy caress that molded her body to his. They traveled from her waist to cup the firm swell of her buttocks. This time, when his knee parted hers, he lifted her toward him until she rode the hard pressure of his thigh. With every lunge of his hips the pressure increased and then retreated, as he made love to her through the barrier of their clothes.

Nothing like this had ever happened to her before. She

felt drugged yet stimulated by his lovemaking. The shock of his hands on her naked waist came as a surprise until she realized that he had pulled her dress up above her hips. And then one hand moved around, across her stomach and up to capture the quivering firmness of a breast.

His movement was deliberate as his thumb circled about the aureole. Each brush of his thumbnail across the infinitely sensitive nipple made her gasp softly as sizzling waves of pleasure shot through her.

"Tell me to stay, Georgie," he begged against her ear. "Tell me, please!"

She heard his voice as if from a long way off. She didn't want words, didn't want the responsibility of any decisions, only the heady excitement that had her gasping in pleasured torment. She wanted him more than she had ever wanted any man in her life. Didn't he know?

"Georgie, say it," Maxim murmured again into her mouth. He could force a yes from her and he knew it. The movement of her hips under his hands was proof that she was more than ready for him. But he had never forced acquiescence from a woman; nor had he ever made love to a woman who had a husband. And, amazingly, he discovered that that was what was stopping him.

Anger flashed through him and he yanked his head back, gasping for breath. She must do this of her own free will.

Losing the ardor of his kiss was like surfacing too suddenly from the depths. Georgianna's head fell forward against his chest.

He reached down and held her face in his fingers,

turning it up to meet his. "I could take the decision out of your hands," he offered with rough urgency.

*But you won't,* she thought, her eyes clouding with pain. "But you won't," she repeated aloud in misery.

For a long moment they stood locked by their gazes, soft brown eyes captured by Dutch-blue. Her body throbbed against his. A single short word held them apart.

"No," Maxim said, releasing her. "I won't."

Had she untied his tie and opened his shirt? She didn't remember doing it. Yet now that he had pushed her away, her mind began recording all kinds of nonsensical details. He was heaving; the broad planes of his exposed chest rose and fell as if under the pressure of a bellows. His hair was mussed, falling across his brow and over his ears. The usually well-defined lines of his mouth were blurred, softened by her kisses. But it was his expression that made her turn away and try unsuccessfully to pull her dress down over her hips with trembling hands.

His expression was taut with frustration and disappointment. She stopped a sob with the palm of her hand. He had every right to be angry. They wouldn't have gone nearly this far if she hadn't encouraged him.

The sudden ringing of the telephone behind her sent Georgianna leaping away with a cry of fright.

Maxim watched her a moment, barely containing the urge to rip the phone out of the wall as it rang a second time. "Answer it, damn it," he shouted at the third shrill ring. When she didn't move, only shook her head, he crossed the room and snatched up the receiver.

"Georgianna! Thank God! Where have you been?"

The male voice acted like a splash of cold water,

draining Maxim in one quick moment of his sexual heat. He turned and held out the receiver. "It's for you," he said dully.

It seemed to Georgianna that she moved in slow motion, that the excruciating moment when the phone was in her hand would never come. "Hello?"

"Georgianna? Who answered the phone?" Alan Byrd demanded. "Are you all right? I've been calling since ten-thirty. Who's that man?"

Georgianna's eyes were on Maxim, so she saw him flinch as his gaze lit on the picture on her nightstand. "I'm fine, really," she said to the man on the line. "I had a fuse blow tonight and had to get help. The repairman answered the phone because I was—well, in the john."

She saw Maxim's head jerk toward her, astonishment in his eyes.

*I'm learning to lie,* she thought with a shiver of revulsion.

"Georgianna, you sound funny," Alan persisted.

"Of course I sound funny," she answered, feeling frightening giggles of hysteria bubbling in her chest once more. She'd nearly made love to a man who thought she was an adulteress.

*Saved by the bell.* Another giggle struggled to be free, almost choking her. "I'll call you back when the repairman's gone," she said quickly, and dropped the receiver back into its cradle.

Maxim picked up the gilt-framed picture of the naval officer and stared at it. "This is Edward," he said to no one in particular. With extreme care he replaced the picture and shrugged his tuxedo jacket back onto his shoulders. Only then did he look at Georgianna.

"You should be more discriminating in your choice of repairmen. An unscrupulous man might have taken advantage of you."

The dead weight of those words wounded. She covered her mouth with a trembling hand. "Go home, Maxim," she whispered. "Go home."

She listened to the heavy measure of his footfalls echoing as he descended the stairway, so different from his usually light tread, and wondered if he were as shattered by the events of the night as she. When the front door closed behind him, she went downstairs and locked it.

The stream of hot water in the shower helped soothe her emotional turmoil and when she was wrapped in her velour robe, she sat in the dark and rocked.

A lot had happened this night, much of it ridiculous and much of it foolish and all of it her fault. Yet there was something that stood out vividly from the rest of the muddle. Something she hadn't even suspected until this night. Was it possible? It made absolutely no sense. And yet the idea remained.

After a long moment she slipped the gold wedding band off her finger and put it in her pocket. She couldn't wear it anymore, that much she was sure of.

*Am I falling in love or simply falling apart?*

# Chapter Ten

"That's it for today!" Frank Howard slumped down on the narrow chrome-and-fake-leather bench that served as a sofa in his office. "We managed to fit that last-minute story in, as you directed," he continued sourly. "It's in the third column on page five. Any other orders, boss?"

Maxim didn't look up from the work on the desk in front of him. Frank's edginess was a reflection of his own. Already they had had two arguments within the hearing of the *Chronicle*'s staff. He didn't want a third to round out the week.

Drumming his fingers on the desk, he tried to concentrate on the proposal he was studying, but the figures swam before his eyes. He'd spent most of the past seventy-two hours in this tiny cell of a room trying to cram two week's work into three days. The lack of sleep was telling on his judgment, but the sooner he got out of

Frank's way—and out of Frank's office—the better it would be for both of them.

"Is this the best John could come up with?" he finally asked, reaching up to rub his temples.

Frank slipped his glasses up to ride his brow. "I don't know what you expect of us, Max. We're a small operation. We depend on those ads for bulk as well as revenue. Cut very many of them and we're back to a single-sheet rag."

Maxim made a sound of disgust. "So that's it, either we're a glorified shopping flyer or a greensheet. In that case, we might as well give the damned thing away!"

Frank wasn't surprised by the violent motion that sent the stack of budget sheets flying. He'd been a witness to Maxim's temper since they were both children. What did surprise him was the haggard look that had crept into his friend's face.

"When did you last eat?" Frank bent to pick up a few of the sheets that landed nearby. "I don't mean carry-out either. And when did you last sleep in your own bed? You've been mutilating yourself with a razor in the men's room for two days that I know of personally. Why?"

Maxim self-consciously touched the cut on his chin. For a tiny abrasion it had bled a great deal. "I'm trying to finish up. I want the holidays off, too," he muttered.

Frank tossed the collected papers back on the desk. "You have plans for the holidays? Good. Where are you going?"

Maxim looked across the desk at his managing editor. "Are you trying to get rid of me?"

"As soon as possible," Frank declared without hesitation. "Your heart's in the right place, Max, but you're trying to force a whole new method of publishing onto a staff that must deal with the reality of day-to-day production. I'm not even convinced we need . . . All right, all right, let's not begin that argument again," he relented when he saw Maxim's dark brows gathering together. "Forget all this for a few days. It'll be here when you return. I guarantee it."

Maxim nodded. "You're right, of course—about it all being here when I return. *I'm* right about the necessity for changes, and you know it."

Frank shrugged and decided to change the topic. "Where are you going? Just curious. Lisa will want to know so that she can moan and groan about how nice it would be if we could get away once in a while. I tell her she should have thought about that before we started a project to repopulate Plowden singlehandedly."

Maxim smiled for the first time that day. "I've wondered why you two went at it with such concentrated effort. Four children in six years. Haven't you ever heard about planned parenthood?"

Frank laughed outright. "Lisa said something about fielding a basketball team when we married. I didn't realize she was going to make me a staunch advocate of *women's* sports."

Maxim smiled. Frank had four daughters. "Maybe you should be thinking of parlaying all that athletic talent into cash. Aren't colleges and universities responding to the demands for more female athletic scholarships these days?"

Frank raised his brows. "You know, I really have no idea. Four daughters to educate, and I haven't even looked into the possibilities of scholarships of any kind. Of course, Sarah is only in first grade. But, come to think of it, she's a natural soccer player. She plays right wing. No reason why she shouldn't be able to compete on the college level if she sticks with it. God knows, I'd never have afforded Dartmouth if I hadn't won a swimming scholarship.''

The two men exchanged an inspired look before Maxim picked up a pen and began writing in quick, impatient strokes. "Who's your best reporter?"

"I am," Frank responded. "But you're not thinking what I think you're thinking."

"I'm thinking it." Maxim grinned. "Look at it this way, you've a vested interest in the story. Start here in Connecticut. If I like what you do, I'll send you down the coast to do a series of articles about colleges located where other De Hoop papers are published."

Frank raised skeptical brows. "Will I have my own by-line?"

Maxim shrugged. "Maybe."

"I'll be paid, aside from my regular salary with the *Chronicle?*"

"More than likely."

"Travel expenses included?"

"Shouldn't be a problem."

"I'll retain the rights to syndicate?"

Maxim turned a jaundiced eye on his managing editor. "You're pushing."

Frank threw his hands up in a gesture of defense. "Just asking, boss, just asking."

"I've been looking for something that will appeal to readers as a local issue and yet be broad enough to attract the corporation's national readership. This story could be it!

"Most parents would like to provide a college education for their children, but funds are a major stumbling block for many of them. A series of these articles will offer them some new avenues to explore. The topic's got everything: the equal opportunities slant, the feminist issue, the controversy over funding, and the philosophy behind present-day collegiate sports."

The contained excitement in Maxim's tone infected Frank. "You may just have hit upon something, Max! Every time you've mentioned broadening the scope of the *Chronicle* I've envisioned us hustling after front-page news. We're not equipped for it. But this, this is topical, but issue-oriented. It just might work."

"It better," Maxim shot back. "Your raise is hanging in the balance. It will mean travel," he warned. "Lisa might not be as eager for you to make a national name for yourself as you might think."

Frank stood up, rubbing his hands. "You leave Lisa to me. She's one game lady. I'm not saying she won't mind the traveling, but, with any luck, I can do a lot of the research work right here." He leaned across the desk, wiggling his fair brows. "It would help if you could get the computer system set up soon."

"The system linking the De Hoop publishing enterprises will be operational by the first of the year," Maxim answered, and offered his hand. "Have we got a deal?"

"You bet!"

Frank stood up and began scooping piles of paper into his briefcase.

"Going home?" Maxim asked, glancing at his watch and seeing that it was long past five o'clock.

Frank nodded. "What about that vacation? Thanksgiving means turkey and visits from grandparents for us old married folks. In your case, it's party time. Where are you and Steph going?"

Maxim looked up, an unreadable expression on his face. "I haven't seen Stephanie since the *Chronicle*'s dinner three weeks ago."

Frank hesitated before saying, "It's none of my business, but am I right in assuming that you're seeing Mrs. Manchester?"

"You're right." Maxim's gaze narrowed. "It's none of your business."

There was a short silence.

"But since you're no doubt repeating rumor, I haven't seen Georgianna since the night of the dinner either."

Frank licked his lips. "Sorry, Max. I didn't mean to insult you."

"What do you mean?"

Frank's gaze dropped before the laser-blue stare. "Forget it. I liked her, that's all. Too bad she's married, huh?"

Maxim didn't answer.

When Frank had shut the door behind himself, Maxim leaned back in his chair. Propping his feet on the desktop, one resting on the other, he laced his fingers together across his eyes.

Images of Georgianna filled his mind as he knew they would. Like a collage of snapshots, they dominated his field of vision: images of her on the beach, at the country fair, in the park, and especially the night of the dance.

How could he ever have thought her less than the most beautiful woman he had ever known? She had shimmered with beauty that night, too alive for his peace of mind.

Because of that, he had crossed the boundary of propriety and had lost even her friendship.

A string of curses erupted from him. He was beginning to think like a puritanical prig. He was no saint, had never aspired to be one. There'd been women, plenty of them. He wouldn't have regretted making love to Georgianna had she been free. Because . . . because . . .

*If Georgianna were free to love him he would marry her.*

The thought came as no surprise, only brought a sadness he'd never before experienced. That was why he hadn't seduced her into the act they had both ached to share. Neither of them would be able to stop with a single night of lovemaking. They wanted each other too badly. They would continue meeting and it would be only a matter of time before everyone guessed. Frank suspected them already. The only way to protect her reputation in a town the size of Plowden was to give no one food for gossip.

The pain that had been tapping softly at his temples all afternoon now hammered Maxim's skull. Placing his palms on either side of his head, he squeezed until the pain eased slightly.

Yet he couldn't leave things between them the way they were. There was something in the equation that didn't add up. She was unhappy. No, more than that. She wasn't the kind of woman to shy at shadows. She'd been terrified, not of the dark, but of what it might conceal.

He sat up so suddenly; his chair skidded back against the wall.

She had not denied that she was unhappily married. She hadn't even answered his questions about running away from her husband. She'd tried to confuse him with her laughter. If there were any chance that her fears stemmed from her marriage, that she was considering leaving her husband, then he had to know.

Once he had been a man attracted by a striking stranger. Even then he'd wanted to make love to her. Now, knowing her and that he mustn't touch her again, his feelings hadn't lessened. But being in her presence would be worth the pain of denying his love for her.

As he walked out of the *Chronicle*'s front door fifteen minutes later, the first hunger pangs he'd felt in two weeks hit him. A quiet dinner for two came to mind. Smiling, he backed his car out of the parking lot and headed toward a nearby fish market. As long as Georgianna was learning to cook, he might as well teach her how to make his favorite dish: broiled lobster.

The first snow of the season was threatening the New England states as Georgianna walked down her driveway. Low, slate-colored clouds filled the sky, making it night at five P.M. on this November afternoon. The air was icy cold, stinging her cheeks and wrists where her gloves didn't quite meet her jacket sleeves. Frost-covered grass crunched under her heels as she walked across the lawn to pick up the evening paper. She never looked at it anymore. Almost daily it featured a picture or article about its publisher Maxim De Hoop. Still, bringing in the paper was part of her job.

She turned back to the house with a sigh. Isolation was more terrible than she'd ever imagined it would be. It was as if the real Georgianna had ceased to exist in the two months since she'd come to live in Plowden. There was never any mail for her, never any phone calls besides Alan's. One day slid into the next without distinction.

The flash of headlights swinging onto the street at the far end didn't catch her attention. It wouldn't be anyone looking for her address.

She paused on the drive as Cora's porch light came on, revealing the harvest decoration of dried corn and gourds hanging on her front door. Thanksgiving was two days away, and she'd have no one to share it with, she reflected sadly. In the morning Cora was going into New York to spend the holiday weekend with old friends. Cora had invited her to come along, but Georgianna knew it was only a kindness.

The flash of headlights on the driveway directly behind her made Georgianna spin around in surprise. Immediately the lights died. The sight of Maxim De Hoop's white Lamborghini sent blood pulsing through her body, but she didn't move. She stood staring stupidly as the car door opened and he slid out of the driver's seat.

Unconsciously she stiffened. Why was he here after three long weeks without a word? He seemed to sense her withdrawal, for he stopped after taking only a step toward her.

"Hello."

His voice was the same, its warm masculine tones reaching out to wrap around her heart. "Hello, Maxim."

His gaze seemed to drink her in as always, absorbing her image as film absorbs the reflection of light.

"How have you been, Georgie?"

She shrugged, beginning to shiver inside her down-filled jacket. "Awful," she finally admitted.

"Me, too."

"Have you kept busy?"

"I've missed you," he answered in an urgent way that did strange things to her breathing pattern.

"It's cold," she said, seeking to read his expression in the dusky light.

"It will be warmer inside," he answered.

"Yes. Warmer."

Neither of them moved. A dozen questions hovered on her lips, but she couldn't speak them.

"I brought some groceries for dinner. Do you mind?" Maxim tensed as he waited for her answer.

She shook her head, and then she smiled. "I've missed you, Maxim."

She saw the shadows alter on his face and knew that he was smiling at her. "I hope you like lobster. I've a pair of lively ones on the seat."

She came up beside him as he bent and leaned into the car's interior. "Here, this is for you," he said, handing back a sack with one hand.

She scooped up the bag, feeling the cold shape of chilled bottles.

"Champagne," he confirmed as he straightened with a bag in his other hand. "To toast our friendship," he added as she stood looking questioningly at him.

She turned away, not really listening, as once more a vehicle turned the corner. Maxim had come back, after she had given up hope of ever seeing him again. The hum of old desire coupled with new notes of her discovered love for him filled her thoughts completely.

Explosive sounds like gunfire shattered the silent street with noise. In that split second Georgianna felt the acute despair of happiness found too late. The next instant the instinct for self-preservation took over.

It seemed to take forever to reach the safety of the ground. The free-falling sensation echoed and re-echoed with the sound of the explosions. It was happening again. They had found her! The shots were meant for her!

Pain ripped through her, corrupting rational thought. Maxim! Maxim was behind her! She could hear him crying out to her. He must be hurt! And somewhere a woman was screaming, screaming as though her life was being torn from her.

Maxim had stopped to lock his door when the noise jarred the street. He looked up as the backfiring motor-cycle roared past, but his disparaging comment was cut off by the horror of a scream.

"Georgianna? Georgianna! Oh, my God!"

She was sprawling facedown on the driveway as though she'd thrown herself flat. It was her scream that chilled his blood as he dropped his bag and raced to her side.

Falling to his knees, he touched a hand to her face. "Georgianna, it's okay," he whispered hoarsely. "I'm here, Georgie. You fell, but you're going to be okay."

"What's wrong?"

Maxim looked up briefly to see Cora Walton hurrying across toward him.

"Georgianna fell," he shouted back, bending over to carefully turn her onto her back. She was half-conscious and gasping because the breath had been knocked out of her. It was then that he saw the blood around the tear in her right sleeve.

"Damn! She's cut herself!" He was grateful that his hands did not shake as he unzipped Georgianna's jacket and pulled it off. Nor did he hesitate when he saw the long jagged gash across her wrist and forearm. It must have been caused by the broken champagne bottles.

"Go get something, a clean rag, a towel, anything I can use to staunch the flow of blood," he directed as Cora reached his side.

As she hurried back toward her house, he applied pressure to the wound, squeezing it shut with his fingers. "It's going to be okay, Georgie. I'm taking care of everything," he crooned against her hair as he held her tightly with his other arm. She didn't answer, only closed her eyes.

It seemed like an eternity before Cora came running back across the lawn. "I brought tea towels; they're clean," she said breathlessly.

"Fold one twice and then apply hard pressure when I remove my hand," he ordered. "Clamp down tight, Cora, she's losing a lot of blood." Folding a second towel, he added it to the one Cora held to the wound. Taking a third, he wound it around Georgianna's arm and tied it.

"There," he said under his breath. Sliding an arm under her legs and another under her shoulders, he lifted Georgianna and rose to his feet.

"I'll call an ambulance."

Maxim looked up in surprise to see several neighbors standing around them. He hadn't heard them come up.

"It'll take too long," he answered. "Take my keys, Cora, and open my car door. The bandage will control the bleeding until we reach the hospital."

Georgianna's head rolled as it lay against his shoulder. "Don't . . . kill me!" she whispered thickly.

"You're all right, baby," he whispered, and kissed her brow. "You hurt yourself but you're safe now. I've just got to get you to the hospital."

When Cora swung the passenger door open, Maxim bent and eased Georgianna's limp body into the seat. After belting her in, he looped the end of his makeshift bandage over the clothes hook to keep her arm elevated.

He ran three stop signs and two red lights as he leaned on his horn and kept his emergency lights flashing. When he pulled into the emergency entrance of Plowden General he was grimly amused to find a patrol car right behind him.

He practically leaped over the hood of his car to open her door. "It's going to be fine, Georgie girl," he assured as she whimpered in pain. "I'll protect you." Scooping her up, he turned toward the hospital entrance.

And then suddenly, there were other hands offering aid, taking her weight from him and carrying her away.

"Good evening, Mrs. Manchester."

Georgianna's lids fluttered, opened to blinding light, and squeezed shut again. The roaring in her ears ebbed and faded, separating into distinct voices and sounds.

"She's coming around. You can get Mister De Hoop," she heard a woman say.

Her heart lurched. Maxim was here? "Maxim?" she whispered to the disembodied voice, but there was no reply. She breathed in, amazed that there was no pain in her chest, and tried again. "Where's Maxim?"

"Right here, baby!"

Again she struggled to open her eyes, and this time she was rewarded with the deep blue of his eyes.

"Maxim," she murmured, a smile softening the stiff corners of her mouth.

"You scared the hell out of me," he said roughly. "Georgianna, what happened?"

Her smile deepened as she stared up unheedingly at the man she loved more dearly than her life. "Did you buy those eyes? Would you buy a pair for me to always remember you by?"

He touched her cheek, as white as the sheet under her head. "You lost over a pint of blood. Guess what? We're the same type."

"Of course," she answered sleepily, her voice seeming to drift away from her. She was floating, not quite touching the ground. "We've always been the same type. If only there weren't so many secrets." She giggled, not quite certain why, but completely relaxed in the knowledge that Maxim was safe.

"Doctor?" Maxim looked uncertainly at the man beside him.

"She's had a shock. The drug we gave her for pain and the anesthetic we used in sewing up her arm are bound to make her woozy. She'll be fine in the morning. Right now the important thing is for her to get some rest. If you will fill out these forms, I can have her admitted."

"I'm not family," Maxim said slowly, wondering how best to handle the situation. Turning to the doctor, he said, "Her husband's name is Edward Manchester. He's a naval officer and out of the country at present. I don't know any next of kin. I'll pay for any services. Just do what is required."

A cool hand slipped into Maxim's and squeezed gently. "Maxim? I want to go home." Georgianna tried to lift her head, found that it felt like extra weight had been added, and gave up the effort. "I want to go home."

"You should spend the night in the hospital, Mrs. Manchester," the doctor answered, moving into her field of vision. "You've lost some blood and you need rest. If you will just help Mister De Hoop fill out these papers and sign this admittance form, we'll have you tucked in for the night in no time."

Georgianna's grip tightened on Maxim's hand as for the first time she realized she didn't know where she was. "Where am I?"

"The emergency room at Plowden General." Maxim frowned down at her. "Don't you remember? You tripped and fell on the driveway. One of the champagne bottles you were carrying broke on the concrete and cut your wrist.'' He gently touched her right arm. ''You've got several dozen stitches here, Georgie.''

Georgianna stared up at him through the confusion of her euphoria. Hadn't there been gunfire? She was certain she'd heard it! ''Only bottles? No bullets?''

The doctor's head swiveled round at Georgianna's remark. ''What'd she say?''

''She must be dreaming,'' Maxim answered quickly. ''The medicine and all.''

But his mind was racing back over the moments before he saw her lying on the drive. There had been the backfire of a motorcycle, sudden and sharp in the stillness. Backfires were sometimes mistaken for gunfire, but why would Georgianna make the connection? His own irritated surprise was a result of the months he'd spent in the Middle East, where loud explosions of shells and bombs might mean sudden death.

Yet, when he'd picked Georgianna up to put her in the car, she had whispered the words that now came screaming back through his thoughts:

*Don't . . . kill me!*

What the hell was going on?

Georgianna had shut her eyes. Thinking was an effort, but one thought was clear. She couldn't tell Maxim that she had deliberately thrown herself to the ground. He wouldn't understand and she couldn't explain it to him. She'd made a terrible mistake. ''I want to go home. Now.''

''Mrs. Manchester, it isn't wise to leave. If you would just—''

''No!''

She was amazed at the volume of her voice. The confidence generated by it seemed to revive her, and she levered herself to a sitting position. Reality swooped back quickly as she swayed like a drunk, almost toppling off the table.

Maxim caught her, bracing her with a hand on each shoulder. She was so weak her muscles trembled from the effort to support her body. "Georgianna, listen to me! You can't go home. You need the best care money can buy."

She raised her head, a lock of hair sweeping her cheek. Her face was drawn and her eyes were dull with pain, but determination edged her husky voice as she said, "You've got money and influence, Maxim. Please, please, get me out of here!"

Maxim's heart went out to the pale and trembling woman beneath his hands. Gently, he laid her back and brushed the tangled hair from her face. "Okay, Georgie, whatever you want." Over his shoulder he asked, "Is it possible to take her home?"

The doctor looked annoyed. "It isn't wise. She's lucid, and that's a good sign. The effects of shock from loss of blood were minimal. But she's in no shape to walk out the door."

Maxim's eyes never left Georgianna's face as he said, "If I carry her, put her in bed and keep her there, is it safe to take her home?"

The doctor hesitated. "The laceration wasn't critical, but it was serious. She'll need constant monitoring. She's had one IV to replace lost fluid. She should have another.'

Maxim nodded. "I'll take you home after that, Georgie," he said tenderly, and received her beautiful smile of thanks.

"Mrs. Manchester will need absolute quiet and lots of fluids," the doctor directed when Georgianna had finished the second IV. "And she'll have to sign a release absolving the hospital of any responsibility. I've filled two prescriptions for her. One's an antibiotic, the other is for pain. She should be watched closely tonight. She could go into shock again if she's not very careful."

"She'll be careful," Maxim said grimly. "I'll see to that."

"What time is it?" Georgianna demanded as the nurse helped her into her clothes.

"Ten P.M."

Five hours lost, Georgianna mused miserably. Alan would have been ringing her phone every fifteen minutes since seven-thirty. How would she explain all this to him? What could she say, *I made a fool of myself because I mistook backfire for someone shooting at me*? Some witness she would make in the courtroom.

Maxim came in when she was buttoned up. "Where's my coat?"

He looked baffled, and then he remembered. "On your front lawn. Use this." He stripped off his fur-lined suede bombardier jacket and laid it about her shoulders.

"You'll be cold," she protested as he scooped her up, but her arms went happily about his neck.

"I have you to keep me warm," he teased. "Let's go. Tom brought the limo, so I don't have to worry about you bouncing around while I drive."

"It's snowing!" Georgianna said in wonder as they stepped out of the emergency room into the night. Lacy white flakes drifted through the light of the parking area. "Beautiful."

"Yes, beautiful," Maxim agreed quietly, his gaze on her face. "You scared the hell out of me, Georgie," he murmured, brushing a quick kiss across her temple. "I don't think I'll ever be able to look at another champagne bottle without thinking of this night."

He stepped into the limo without releasing her and then sat with her across his lap, shielding her with his body as they rode.

She melted against him. He was so warm she had the urge to wriggle down even closer to him, but she didn't dare. The light touch of his hands, holding her as if she would shatter, was a welcome caress. The firm curve of his muscular body against her quickened her pulse. If she shifted closer to him she knew he'd realize the disturbing effect his nearness was having on her. She'd thought she would never be this close to him again. Yet, miracle of miracles, it was happening. It almost made the past hours worth it.

Lifting her left hand, she touched the nick on his chin. She'd noticed it in the emergency room, and it was so unlike him that she had marveled at it. "Who cut you, Maxi-millions?" she whispered.

He chuckled. "Where'd you get that name for me?"

She shrugged sleepily, drowsiness slurring her words. "I made it up . . . weeks ago."

"You must have been thinking about me." His voice had grown heavy with an emotion she couldn't quite identify.

"I think . . . about you," she answered in the barest whisper.

Maxim knew a moment of utter contentment, the first he had experienced in many months. Suddenly everything was clear. He and Georgianna had a future. Somehow, some way, things would work out for them. He believed that now.

"Someone's there!" Georgianna murmured as they pulled up before the Rhoadses' house. Lights blazed from the living-room windows and from her bedroom on the second floor.

"It's Cora. I called her from the hospital to tell her that you were okay," Maxim explained. "You scared all of us." He hugged her in a tender squeeze. "She said she'd be here when we got home. You need someone to look after you."

"But I thought—" Georgianna caught herself too late. She saw it in Maxim's face.

"You want me to stay with you," he stated. "What about Cora, and everyone else? Your reputation will be ruined." He said it with just enough humor in his voice so that she couldn't be hurt.

"What if . . . I don't care?"

Maxim studied her face. She was exhausted, hurt, and still drugged. He mustn't act on anything she said this night. "Don't tempt a man, Georgie. I'll take a rain check when you're in better condition to defend yourself."

"Maxim! Georgianna! I was so worried!" Cora greeted them as Maxim carried his patient into the hallway. "The bed's already turned back. Would you like some tea or soup, Georgianna?"

"Just bed," Georgianna muttered against Maxim's shoulder as he carried her up the steps to the second floor.

As they entered the bedroom, the phone rang. He bent and laid her across the bed while Cora picked it up.

"Yes. She's just arrived," Cora answered, and then placed her hand over the mouth piece. "Georgianna, there's a young man on the phone for you. He's called three times already. He says he's your brother."

Georgianna's gaze slid from Maxim's. That would be Alan. "I'll talk to him."

Her two companions exchanged glances, but neither of them offered to leave the room and give her privacy.

"Hello, Alan." Georgianna's voice was a soft mumble. "No . . . nothing serious. I tripped . . . cut myself. Yes, pints of blood." She giggled. "I'm kidding, Alan. Tired, very tired. I don't . . . no hospitalization. I need sleep. Call you tomorrow." Without waiting for Cora to hang up the phone, she shut her eyes, half asleep already.

"If you'll put on her nightgown, I'll wait downstairs," Maxim suggested. Cora nodded.

Ten minutes later Cora's steps sounded on the stairs. Maxim jumped up from his seat before the fireplace and met her in the hall.

"She's sleeping soundly. Poor dear, she wouldn't let me call anyone. And I certainly didn't feel it was my place to suggest that her brother come here."

The frown of concern on Cora's face worried Maxim. "Did something bother you about him, Cora?"

For a moment Cora looked reluctant to speak, as if she'd spoken out of turn. "No, not really. But he was quite rude when I said Georgianna wasn't here, that she'd been hurt. I haven't heard such language since I quit teaching!''

Maxim's smile wasn't warm. ''Perhaps he was just worried about his sister.''

''Perhaps,'' Cora conceded.

Maxim's gaze lifted to the ceiling, the hair rising on the back of his neck. Georgianna was in danger. He could feel it. And the man called Alan was connected with it.

''You're worried about her,'' Cora said.

''She's had a rough night,'' Maxim answered, deliberately hiding his thoughts. ''I promised the doctor that someone would stay with her all night.''

Cora nodded. ''I will do that. Though, to be honest, she made me promise to go home after I locked up. She can be very stubborn. I'll just putter about down here. She'll never know I'm here unless she wakes up and needs me.''

Maxim wasn't listening. If Georgianna was involved in some kind of danger, Cora would never be able to protect her.

''I think it would be better if I stayed here tonight.'' He blushed under Cora's gray gaze like a schoolboy caught red-handed. ''Don't misunderstand. We're not lovers. But I do love her.''

''She's a very unhappy young woman,'' Cora said after a moment, her gaze hard on Maxim's face. ''I don't know if I should say this, but I believe she feels the same way you do. I don't approve of marriages breaking up, but, if you ask me, there's nothing to destroy in this case. I'll go home.''

When the door closed behind Cora, Maxim made a quick tour of the house, locking up and shutting off the lights.

Finally, upstairs, he pulled Georgianna's rocker over to her bedside and sat down.

Cora had helped her exchange her bloody clothes for a blue flannel gown with ruffled collar and cuffs. Lying in the circle of the lamplight, she looked very young and very vulnerable. She was so still he touched her closest wrist to find the pulse. After he found it, it seemed natural to continue to hold her hand.

"Georgie, Georgie, you've got to trust me," he murmured as he bent and kissed her wrist.

# Chapter Eleven

The painkillers had done their work. There was no more throbbing in Georgianna's arm. But the painful images of her dreams were another matter.

She was in a long hallway, a tunnel tapering away from her into infinity. Overhead a bare bulb hung from a cord. Panicky thoughts whirled through her mind. There was danger here. She must get away!

But when she turned there was no door behind her. Nothing. She ran her fingers over the solid white surface. A wall. Turning back, she faced the tunnel again.

And then she saw them.

They were only shadows, three tall square-shouldered silhouettes beyond the stairway. Her mouth worked spasmodically, forming words without sound or expression as she clawed the glassy surface of the wall.

A cry went up from one of the men, a hiss of expletives that jerked her head around. The explosion of the pistol sounded like a cannon blast, jarring her teeth as the barrel erupted in a slow-motion nightmare of flame and sparks.

Suddenly, she faced the miracle of a doorway. She flung herself against it. Stumbling into the street, she again heard herself hailed with filthy words.

RUN! RUN!

It was the only thought in her mind, yet her legs wouldn't work. The pavement had softened under her feet, becoming a sticky oozing tar that sucked at her shoes.

The terrifying noise of a pistol shot, fired at close range, pushed her down. Or was it the force of a bullet?

Pain exploded down her right arm as she hit the hard, unyielding stretch of concrete.

*Oh my God! He's going to kill me!*

"Oh, God! He's trying to kill me!"


"Georgianna! Georgianna! Wake up. It's only a dream. Georgianna?"

Maxim lifted her up, thwarting her attempts to break free as she pounded him with weak fists.

"Georgie girl, it's okay. It's only Maxim." Holding her firmly about the shoulders, he caught her bandaged arm and forced her hand against the bristly contour of his cheek. "Feel me, Georgianna. I'm real."

It was too dark to see, but suddenly Georgianna knew the voice speaking to her. "Maxim?"

"Georgie! Thank God!" He pulled her against him,

wrapping his arms tightly about her to rock her gently as sobs broke from her lips. "Shh, baby. It was only a nightmare. While I'm here nothing can hurt you. I swear it! Nothing can hurt you."

After a moment her crying lessened and he gathered her closer, lifting her into his lap. She was shivering from cold and the after-effects of her nightmare. Tears of anger stung his eyes. Whoever had done this to her would pay. "God, Georgie, what happened to you?"

Lifting her face to meet his he began kissing the salty tears from her cheeks. He felt her arms about his neck. At least she knew him. The first tentative kisses he pressed at the corner of her mouth brought a murmur from her. With a small movement of her head she brought her lips under his.

He captured her soft mouth and blended their lips in kiss after kiss.

Georgianna felt the tension easing from her, forced out by the stronger emotion of desire. With one arm about her waist, he held her securely to his chest while his free hand stroked her from shoulder to hip. Luxuriating in the incredibly sweet feel of his body, she arched to meet the subtle pressure of his hand.

When she turned away from his kiss to touch her mouth to the heated skin of his neck, a groan of pleasure issued softly from his lips. "Love me, Maxim. Make love to me," she whispered into his ear.

"Oh, Georgie." Maxim sighed. When her hand moved tentatively to his chest, he closed his eyes. Her fingers moved slowly, searching out the masculine contours of his body. The spidery touch made his pulse leap and throb, but still he did not move to turn her on her back as he ached to do. He ground his teeth and waited.

After what seemed an eternity, the touching ceased and her hand settled lightly, palm up, in his lap.

"Georgianna?"

She had fallen asleep.

But even in sleep she wouldn't release him. When he rose to lay her back down, her arm locked about his neck, urging him down on the bed beside her.

"Please," she mumbled, turning instinctively into his warmth as he stretched out beside her. "Good." She sighed, rubbing her body against the long length of his.

"Yes, good," he repeated, a little wryly. "But I'd be lying, Georgie girl, if I didn't say it could be a lot better!"

Georgianna awakened to the sensation of warmth. It was heat that touched every inch of her back from neck to toes and then spread across her waist to her stomach as she lay on her side. It was the most pleasant awakening she could remember. Not wishing to hasten the inevitable moment when she must rise, she didn't even open an eye.

Most mornings she woke to find herself in a tight ball. One false move and her foot or hand would slide into the frozen territory of unwarmed sheets.

Yet this morning she was lying fully stretched out, every muscle unbelievably relaxed. The room was bright, she could tell that even without opening her eyes. It would be midmorning. Was it summer? No, it was winter. The heavy cocoon of warmth pressed around her must be a pile of blankets.

A languorous stretch accompanied by a faint sigh brought reality back. A dull pain shot up her right wrist as she met the imprisoning barrier of a large arm.

Even as she turned toward it, the arm lifted slightly, allowing her to roll onto her back. Opening her eyes, Georgianna stared up into the heavy-lidded, slumberous blue gaze of Maxim De Hoop.

"'Morning."

His voice was thick with sleep, but his eyes were kindling with the light of awareness as he leaned over her. A blue shadow of beard covered his face, and dark hair fell forward onto his brow. The same dark hair curled in fine corkscrews across the expanse of his chest.

Her gaze moved slowly down his bronzed torso until the elastic band of his briefs came into view. That was all he wore, navy-blue briefs. Now she became aware that her gown had ridden up nearly to her waist. Without even realizing it, she let her big toe glide up and down the calf of his hair-roughened leg in an unconscious act of seductive pleasure.

As if he could read her mind, he braced himself on an elbow and reached out to enclose her hip, searing the naked skin with the heat of his palm as he rolled her toward him. When they were touching from shoulder to knee, she could feel the heavy hot throbbing of his manhood against her through the thin barrier of his garment.

He smiled, "You do this to me every time I think of you." His lips went to her cheek and then his tongue found her scar and traced it.

"I love this little imperfection. It makes you real, Georgie. And . . . I . . . want . . . you . . . real," he murmured, punctuating his words with flicks of his tongue into the swirl of her ear.

Georgianna shut her eyes, overwhelmed by the sensation of his touch. All the heat was now inside her. If he kissed her, she knew she would erupt in liquid flames.

Her thighs trembled on his and a gasp of involuntary pleasure parted her lips as his hand curved over the firm swell of her bottom, urging her hard against him.

"Love me, Georgie! Love me!" he begged in rough need.

"I do!" she murmured huskily. "Oh, Maxim, I do love you!"

She didn't stop to think. The sensual accord between them was rooted in something much, much more. They had been aware of one another for months, denying, circling, testing, unable to believe that something as natural and necessary as love could begin from such primitive feelings. She had been taught to distrust, to deny the animalistic urges of her sexual being until other, more civilized criteria had been met. In all her life, the two had never been one. But now she knew that *this* was meant to be, that rules are sometimes broken by exceptional need. And her love for Maxim was an overwhelming need.

She didn't realize immediately that he was pulling away from her. She thought he was simply adjusting himself to make love to her. It wasn't until he sat up and swung his legs over the side of the bed that she knew he was backing off.

"What's wrong?" She tried to push herself upright, only to cry out in pain as she put weight on her bandaged arm.

Maxim swung around and took her in his arms. "Easy, Georgie. The doctor said you were to spend a few days in bed." With a calm efficiency that hurt her, he pressed her gently back against the pillows and covered her up.

She gazed up at him in disbelief. "Didn't you hear what I said?" she whispered, caught between embarrassment and her need to know.

"I heard," he answered softly. There was pain in his voice. "We can't do this, not with . . ." His eyes went to the nightstand, but Edward's picture wasn't there. His brows rose in surprise. He couldn't recall seeing it the night before, either.

Georgianna knew what he was thinking, and she pulled her left hand out from under the covers and held it before him. The wedding band was gone.

Maxim stared at her hand for a full minute and then reached out to bring it to his lips for a quick kiss.

Then he shook his head, as if denying an inner struggle. "We must talk, Georgianna. There are things that must be settled first."

"Now!" she urged, reaching for his hand. But again he shook his head, moving out of her reach.

"You've been through a lot. I'll make you some breakfast. You rest." He picked up her cup from the nightstand and went across the hall into the bathroom. When he returned he had two pills and fresh water. "Take these," he ordered, dropping the pills into her palm.

When she had swallowed them he put down the cup and reached for his slacks and shirt.

She watched him, marveling at how naturally he moved through the world with or without clothes. "I love you," she repeated when he reached the door.

He turned, the tenderest smile yet on his face. "I know."

She didn't go back to sleep. The ache in her arm only served to underscore the feeling that she'd made a complete mess of her life during the past few months. She'd always been so busy, so determined to make up for lost time, that she had not even stopped to wonder where she was heading. The auto accident had cost her a year of schooling. Could she accept that? No. She'd gone to school year round for three years in order to make up the lost credits and graduate with her class. And then she'd jumped into law school with no breather for three more grueling years of study and work. Passing the bar on her first try, she'd signed up to help the poor and neglected. Estacio had been a challenge that she couldn't deny. That was why she had gone heedlessly into his neighborhood and wound up nearly getting herself killed.

And it didn't stop even then. She'd been eager, almost gleeful in her desire to do her civil duty. A criminal wanted her silenced? She was up to any challenge. She would simply change towns, change her name and . . .

"Ruin my life," she muttered angrily. She hadn't expected to meet a man. She hadn't had time for much dating and romance in the last six years. None of the men she had met interested her enough to make her want to slow down, to be with them, to maybe chance falling in love.

Until Maxim.

And now there were so many half-truths and outright lies between them he would probably walk out the door and never speak to her again when she did tell him what was going on.

"But you can't. Not yet."

She rolled over onto her stomach and buried her head under a pillow. She was still in hiding. Nothing would alter that until the trial—if the man out on bail even appeared.

She groaned, burrowing deeper into the dark cavern. She was neatly caught between her sense of duty to Alan and the system of justice of which she was a part, and her bursting love for Maxim De Hoop. Perhaps, if she told him her secret, he would understand. And, if he understood he would . . . insist on protecting her.

That thought popped Georgianna's head up from between the pillows. Maxim would want to be with her constantly, looking after her, spinning a cocoon of safety about her. But the reality of it was that he would be putting himself in jeopardy for her sake. Nothing had happened yet, but she couldn't shake the sense of impending danger. It rode her constantly.

She smoothed her hand over the white bandage wrapped from her palm midway to her elbow. That sense of peril had made her jump to the wrong conclusion the night before. If she had to worry about anyone else, or—God forbid—if something should happen to Maxim because of her, she would be lost.

No, she couldn't tell Maxim the truth. Not yet. So how to make him believe that she really and truly loved him?

Lying and sitting in bed, she felt strong and capable. Once her feet hit the floor, she experienced the full potency of the medicine Maxim had given her. Hanging onto every bit of furniture between the bed and the doorway, she inched toward the hall. They weren't lovers yet. She couldn't ask him to carry her into the bathroom.

Breakfast was one of Maxim's favorite meals. The fact that Georgianna's refrigerator contained only two eggs, milk, and three oranges didn't faze him. He was certain that miracles could be performed. When the pantry yielded canned apples and the freezer an untouched rasher of Canadian bacon, he began to smile.

Thirty minutes later, Georgianna edged haltingly into the kitchen, the aromas of cinnamon, sizzling meat, and coffee having drawn her downstairs. She expected to find Cora at the range.

Instead, Maxim stood there, fork in hand, a white apron tied about his waist.

"You!" she exclaimed in surprise.

"If you promise to sit quietly, I'll let you stay down here. Otherwise, it's back to bed," Maxim admonished gently as he slipped an arm about her waist and guided her to the table.

"I couldn't do much with my hair," she mumbled defensively as he gazed down at her.

"You look good enough to eat," he answered lightly, but there was nothing innocent about the look on his face.

She held very still, hoping he would give her the kiss his gaze promised, but he released her after a quick brush of his lips on her forehead.

Breakfast was one delightful surprise after another. The first cup of coffee was wonderfully rich and smooth, confirming her belief that coffee made by someone else is always better than your own. Then came orange juice, freshly squeezed. After that, Maxim pulled his *pièce de résistance* out of the oven: an apple-puff pancake.

They said almost nothing to one another. His smile was tantalizing, but he offered no real clue to his thoughts as he watched her eat. Minute by minute Georgianna's patience drained, until the moment he stood up to clear their plates and she could stand it no longer.

"Why don't you say something? Anything is better than this silence," she complained. "You never minced words before, Maxim De Hoop. Let me have it!"

Very deliberately Maxim set the dishes in the sink and then turned to her with a smile of laughter.

Georgianna didn't see this. The moment he continued toward the sink, she'd risen to leave. The touch on the back of her neck sent a delicious shiver of joy down her spine. His hands moved to her shoulders, turning her toward him, and she leaned her weight against him.

"You know we can't go on like this, Georgie," he said, resting his chin on her bent head.

She nodded. "I know."

"We're going to have to do something about us."

She wasn't certain she heard correctly over the roaring in her ears. "Us?"

"Us," he confirmed.

"What?"

His hand cupped the back of her head. "Tell me about Edward."

Georgianna made a slight movement of denial with her head. She didn't want to expand on the lies already between them.

"Did he try to kill you, Georgie?"

Her head snapped up. "What?"

"You said last night in your nightmare, 'He's trying to kill me.' Is it Edward you're afraid of?" His mouth tightened in anger. "Did he hurt you, beat you, Georgie?"

She gaped at him in stunned amazement. "No! It's nothing like that. I—I made a mistake, the whole thing, being Mrs. Manchester, all of it."

"Do you love him, Georgie?"

Her heart catapulted into her throat. He was waiting, watching her with his soul in his eyes. Her gaze shifted sideways. What could she say? "No, I don't love Edward Manchester. I never did."

His hands tightened on her shoulders until she cringed with the pain. Instantly the grip eased. "Why did you marry him, Georgie? Tell me!"

She looked up at him and knew she could lie no more. "If I tell you I made big mistakes, unnecessary mistakes, which I'm sorry to the bottom of my heart for having made, would you understand?"

She saw the change first in his eyes, those lovely porcelain-blue eyes that seemed to hold an ocean of feeling in their depths. They shimmered like still water with secret deep currents feeding it. And then came his smile. She felt herself opening inside, becoming vulnerable to this man she had resisted for so long.

"Leave him, Georgie."

Shivers danced on her skin. "I can't free myself. Not yet. There's something I must do first."

"Face him?" The edge of anger had crept back into his voice.

It trembled on her tongue to simply tell him. It would be so easy. She could see now how simple and easy it would be. Maxim was a man who knew danger, had earned his living in the midst of violence and upheaval. But none of that was of her doing and nothing would ever threaten him again if she could help it.

She caught his face in her hands, pleased by the rough stubble of his beard which abraded her palms. "I love you, Maxim. I love you. Trust me a little longer. Please."

He held himself away from her. "How long?"

"A few months."

His fingers touched her cheek. "I want you, Georgie. I want you very, *very* badly. That's what we've got to do something about. Very soon."

Georgianna could hardly stand to face the heat of his gaze, and yet she reveled in it. "Now?" she dared to whisper.

His grin made her stomach flip-flop. "With Cora Walton bound to walk in on us? She's been over once already." He stroked her temples with his fingers, feeling the pulse beneath the soft skin. "We'll go away somewhere. I've got a few days' vacation. We'll go up to Vermont. My family has a little place up near the mountains."

He bent, replacing his fingers with his lips. "It's quiet . . . it's secluded . . . it's perfect."

"Cora is going into Manhattan for the Thanksgiving holidays," Georgianna whispered breathlessly as his hands slid forward to untie her robe. "She's supposed to leave today. If we leave after she does, we'll have three whole days with no one to miss me. Oh!"

His fingers had unerringly found the shape of her breasts through her gown and were gently squeezing. "I wanted to strangle Cora last night," he said quietly. "I had envisioned how it would be when I brought you here, when I undressed you myself. I wanted that pleasure very much."

She couldn't answer. Her entire being was focused on the mesmerizing action of his hands' gentle kneading. When the stroking brought the tender swelling of her nipples to his attention, he took them between his thumb and forefinger and squeezed. A moan of sheer desire shuddered through her and her head rolled forward onto his chest.

"I'm going to enjoy Vermont as I never have before," he whispered against the exposed skin of her nape. "Oh yes, I am."

"I'll go," she said, her voice a mere whimper of assent.

After what seemed an eternity, his hands left her breasts and wandered to her shoulders to hold her a little away. When she raised her head, he was smiling at her. "Don't you want to know?"

"What?" she asked dazedly.

"How much I love you."

# Chapter Twelve

*G*eorgianna kept her eyes glued to the red taillights of the car just ahead. Snow flurries like those of two days earlier had begun, and she didn't want to be delayed. She grimaced as a twinge of pain shot up her arm. She'd refrained from taking anything stronger than aspirin because she had to drive. Maxim's anxiety over her ability to maneuver her car was superseded only by his desire that they not be seen leaving together with bags packed. She'd had to argue and argue to keep him from calling off their weekend. Finally, he'd agreed, the frustration in his voice matching her own.

She'd never thought of Maxim as a man who would have second thoughts. His concern for her reputation would have seemed comic if it were not so sincere. After all, in the beginning he had pursued her with alarming disregard for her feelings. But things were different now.

*He loves me!*

Georgianna smiled. She was up to any plan that would gain them a few days of peace and solitude. Besides, she didn't have to drive far—only ten miles. Maxim had planned things so quickly and efficiently that she was in awe. He'd made arrangements for her to leave her car in the very next town. He'd told the garage owner that he was meeting someone and that they would return for the car on Sunday afternoon.

Fifteen minutes after pulling out of her driveway in Plowden, she turned into the driveway of the auto shop in Danbury, Connecticut.

Maxim was already there, as she had known he would be, and her heart went out to him. Standing on the drive dressed in jeans, worn hiking boots, a teal-blue sweater showing at the neck of his suede parka, he was the embodiment of all her best dreams and desires. He didn't wait for her to get out, but snatched the door open, thrusting his head inside.

"Are you okay?"

She smiled brightly, the anxiousness in his voice melting her heart. "I love you."

He looked back quickly over his shoulder and then smothered her in a hard embrace, forcing a brief kiss on her unresisting mouth.

"You're cold," he said accusingly, holding on to her.

She laughed. "Aren't you afraid someone will see us?"

He frowned, remembering his act of caution. "I'm not ashamed to be seen with you."

She nodded. "I know. You just want to protect me."

She placed a mittened hand on his cheek. "Can we go now?"

He grinned. "Just try and stop us!"

Two minutes later, she was leaning back in comfort in his car. He had already packed her clothes and carried them out of her home the night before in grocery bags. She chuckled at the memory.

"What's funny?" He shot her a loving glance.

"Oh, I was just thinking of the last twenty-four hours. This trip has a lot in common with an episode from 'I Spy'."

"That bothers you," he said reaching for her hand, which she readily gave him. "You don't like lies and deceit. I'm sorry."

*If only you knew, my love.* Pangs of conscience swept her. Here he was apologizing for a deception she heartily endorsed, while she sat beside him trapped in a world of lies.

"It isn't that," she said slowly. "I know that deceptions are sometimes necessary. In fact," she squeezed his hand, "so far, you've laid down all the rules and plans. I have a few conditions of my own."

He glanced at her, his dark brows arched in question.

Georgianna gazed ahead, her fingers hard around his. "You mustn't question me about anything to do with Plowden or my situation."

"Edward, you mean," he said coolly.

She nodded. "In part. Promise me, no matter what happens between us, no questions. Please?"

He sighed. "Okay. I want this to be our weekend."

"And no questions about Alan either."

His fingers opened on her hand, but Georgianna didn't let go. She brought his gloved hand up to her cheek and held it. "Please," she whispered again, turning her face to touch her lips to his exposed wrist.

His fingers clenched over hers and he pulled her hand to his mouth to return the tender caress, adding the erotic stimulation of his tongue. "Georgie, I'm trying very hard to do this your way," he murmured. "But I'm bursting with curiosity, and you can't blame me for it."

"No," she agreed softly. "It's too much to expect you to trust me when I can't confide in you."

For the space of a dozen heartbeats only the smooth purr of the engine filled the car.

"Do you want to be with me?" he asked finally.

"More than anything!" she answered, her heart thudding against her ribs.

"Then nothing else really matters, does it?"

"Alan's not my lover," she offered in a whisper.

His head swiveled toward her and the car swerved suddenly, jerking his attention back as he bit off an obscenity. Moments later, he pulled off onto the shoulder of the road. Setting the brake, he turned to face her.

"We'd better finish this conversation here before we get killed."

Georgianna touched the harsh frown lines at his brow. "Isn't that what you've been thinking, Maxi-millions?"

He didn't answer that question, but posed one of his own. "I've been wondering about your nickname for me. Does my wealth bother you?"

"Of course." She followed one frown line down to his nose with her finger. "I don't think I want to be that

well-off. It would make me feel guilty because I hadn't
done anything to earn it.''

''You would have married me,'' he answered, the
lines easing at last.

''That's hardly a recommendation,'' she replied prim-
ly, her finger pressing the tip of his nose. ''That would
make me a gold digger, an interloper, a—''

Stopping her speech with a hand at her mouth, he
added, ''And my wife.''

*Maxim's wife!* She wanted that so much the thought
made her ache.

His lips caught hers unprepared, but only for an
instant. The next moment their mouths and tongues
melded in a mutual caress.

''Well, it seems that settles that problem,'' he said in
breathless satisfaction when he lifted his mouth from
hers.

''There's one other thing,'' Georgianna ventured.
''It's the most important of all.'' He groaned, but she
continued. ''After this weekend, I don't want you to try
to see me again. I mean it. You mustn't come by the
Rhoadses' house or even call.''

''This tryst has more preconditions than a Geneva
Convention,'' he muttered. His hands tightened on the
steering wheel in exasperation. ''Why, if I may ask, is
that stipulation necessary?''

Georgianna stared out at the flakes of snow which
were beginning to gather on the windshield. ''I won't be
in Plowden much longer.'' From the corner of her eye
she saw his head turn toward her, but she kept her eyes
on the swirling bits of white. ''Once I am free I'll call
you, if you still want me.''

"How long will it be before I hear from you?"

She shrugged. One moment she was so warm she thought she would catch fire. Now she was so cold she could hardly remember his heat. "I don't know. It could be weeks."

"Months?" he prompted in irritation.

"Oh, I hope not."

She didn't feel the tears slipping down her cheeks; her face was too numb with cold. But Maxim saw them and could not bear her unhappiness, even if it meant he must see his own desire thwarted.

It really was the most incredible thing, she decided as his arms slid around her, but she was never cold when Maxim touched her.

"You're an enigma, Georgianna, and I don't react well to frustration of any kind," he admitted as his arms strained about her, half-pulling her into his lap.

After several minutes, when the windshield was completely obscured by snow, she drew back from his kiss with a cat-who-ate-the-cream expression. "You don't really want me to ease your frustrations right here, do you?"

"Would you?" Sometime in the last minutes his hands had unzipped her coat and found the curves of her breasts beneath her bulky sweater.

"Is that your desire?" she asked in turn, keeping her eyes quite steady on his.

"My desire is to have you sprawled naked in my bed, your hair spread upon my pillow, and your thighs parted in invitation."

Georgianna looked over his shoulder. "You don't have much of a backseat."

"You're blushing!" he exclaimed in delight. "Georgie, I'm so glad I took a walk on Fairfield Bay that day."

After a quick kiss they parted as if by mutual consent, strapping on their seatbelts.

"What were you doing at Fairfield Bay that day?" she asked when he had pulled back into the traffic on Interstate 84.

"Taking pictures."

"Of what?"

"Of people and things, but mostly—" he grinned— "of you!"

She sat up a little straighter. "Of me? Really? Why?"

His expression became sly. "You have your secrets, I have mine. Maybe, if you're a good girl, there'll be a surprise for you when we get back."

She gave him a dirty look. "You're being unfair."

He shrugged. "I can't talk about you or even ask any questions. That leaves us with a problem. What are we going to talk about on the drive up?"

"You, of course. I know almost nothing about you."

"What would you like to know?"

She settled back into her seat. He was the kindest, dearest person in the world when he wanted to be. "Tell me about your life. Did you enjoy being a photo journalist?"

"Yes and no."

"Is this going to be a game of twenty questions?"

He laughed. "All right. I wanted to be a photo journalist from the moment I first held a camera in my hands. I must have been about eight. It was a Christmas present, the inexpensive snapshot kind. Oh, yes, not everything I was given was embarrassingly grand. My parents taught me to appreciate money. I worked my way through college, waited tables at summer resorts, that kind of thing.''

"Those tables were in Newport or Martha's Vineyard, I'll bet," she chimed in.

"Do you want to hear my story or not?"

She looked smug. "It was Martha's Vineyard!"

He groaned. "I worked, that's the important thing. I have two younger brothers, Gus and Nik. Nik is a foreign correspondent for the *Times* and Gus raises quarter horses in Kentucky with his wife and kids.''

"Do they look like you?"

He glanced at her. "Thinking about shopping around?"

"Nik, what's that short for?"

"Nikolas, in deference to a great-grandmother who was Greek."

"And Gus?"

"Gustave."

"He's the blond," Georgianna said sagely. "And Nik must be tall, dark, and very intense.''

"I'm not jealous, understand, but how would you describe me?"

She propped her hand on her chin, appearing to study his profile intently. "As the eldest, you've worked the hardest, tried to live up to the family's expectations. You're serious to a fault, have always held the most difficult and idealistic dreams. And now you're feeling tied down by circumstance.''

There was a pause before he said, "If you weren't on

my side, I'd be worried. You can read my mind, Georgie.''

"Not really," she answered. "I could be talking about myself. I'm the eldest, too. I've a brother and a sister."

"I've been told about Alan." He winked at her. "Tell me about baby sis. Is she as adorable as you?"

"Maris is nineteen and in Indonesia with my parents. My brother is twenty-one and works for an electronics company on the West Coast." She paused. "His name is James."

"Is Maris blond or dark?"

Georgianna exhaled a sigh. He hadn't asked about Alan. "She's gorgeously blond, a real surfer girl who spends most of her time in bikinis at one beach or another. Dad says she's driving the Indonesian men wild."

He grinned wolfishly. "I think I'm going to like this family of yours."

"Do you miss traveling the world?"

"Keeping me on the track, hmm? Honestly, no. At least, I don't miss what I did the last year. I once thought that, to be important, my work had to reflect all that was wrong with the world, to make people sit up and take notice. Whether it repelled them or made them cry, at least they weren't indifferent to the misery and suffering around them.

"I know now that that was naive. People can be both better and worse than that. There are those who can bawl their eyes out over the corpse of a three-year-old child on the front page, turn the page over, and then gripe about the exorbitant price of foreign aid.

"Then there are others, legions of decent people who help when and where they can. They feel helpless to change things on the world scale but they make a big difference. It's their small contributions that keep the world going on a day-to-day basis."

She smiled at him. He was talking to her like she was a friend, a friend with whom he was at ease sharing confidences. "You're a nice man."

He reached out to squeeze her knee. "Is that why you love me, because I'm a pushover?"

"I love you because you have the head of a realist with the heart of a romantic."

"Are you certain it's not the other way around?"

Georgianna shrugged. "Either way, I like it. So what will you do? Are you being forced to give up photo journalism in order to run the family enterprise?"

"I was looking for an out," he admitted. "I'm only sorry it was provided by my father's death."

She nodded. "I'm sorry, too."

He looked over at her, a quick searing glance that she felt all the way to her toes. "I can't believe you're here beside me." His gravelly tone didn't quite hide the emotion in his voice.

On a lighter note, he said, "You didn't seem surprised that I knew first aid the other night. Would you like to know how I learned it?"

Georgianna adopted his relaxed tone. "I want to know everything about you."

The miles seemed to whiz past as he talked, or maybe, thought Georgianna, she didn't really notice the miles at all. Maxim's experiences in the war-torn zones of the world were horrifying glimpses of a life she could hardly imagine. And yet, interspersed with the agony were glimpses of the spirit of people who must endure the unendurable.

When they stopped for lunch at an inn near Brattleboro, Vermont, she could contain her inspiration no longer.

"Have you thought of compiling a book of your stories? You tell them so well, Maxim, I'm certain you could find a publisher for them. Together with your pictures, the ones you say you kept because they were too maudlin or 'cute' for the newswires, you'd have a convincing, powerful presentation of the other side of war."

He shrugged aside her idea. "Everybody who can spell his name is writing a book."

"But you're the exception. You've got the credentials, you're a trained journalist. The pictures are eloquent statements on their own."

He laughed out loud. "You've never even seen them."

"You've won awards for your work. They'll be wonderful."

"Your loyalty overwhelms me." Grinning, he gestured toward her clam chowder. "Now eat. I want you strong and rested this evening. I have plans for you."

Georgianna chewed the tender clams and potatoes, thinking that even food was better when shared with him.

"Aren't you worried about the weather?"

He looked toward the windows, where snowflakes fell

lightly. "We're going to cross the Green Mountains here in the southern part of the state using the Molly Stark Trail to Bennington. That will be the toughest going. After that, it's north on the New England Heritage Trail past Danby almost to Tinmouth. My place is on an offshoot of the Otter River."

"It sounds like heaven," she sighed.

"It'll be just you and me," he warned. "We could get snowed in."

"Promises, promises," she answered airily, a little afraid of the swelling feeling of happiness in her chest.

"Finish your lunch," he directed. "The distance isn't far, but the weather won't help. I want us there before dark."

Filled with clam chowder and a rum toddy that Maxim insisted she drink because she had refused to take her medication for pain, Georgianna found herself drifting off to sleep not long after they returned to the road.

"Georgie? Darling? Georgie?"

A gentle shake of her shoulder brought her gradually back to consciousness. The first sight her eyes met was Maxim's handsome face hovering above her. A smile eased over her features. "You're really beautiful," she said softly.

His face was so close she saw his pupils expand until his eyes appeared nearly black. "If you knew what I was thinking, you'd run away," he answered.

Sleep had emboldened her. "Why?" she asked, draping her good arm about his neck.

"Because I've wanted you so long and so much, and now you're here, mine at last. I want you. All ways,

Georgie. Every way I can think of. And some I may invent with you here for inspiration.''

"Mmm," she said, lifting her mouth for his kiss.

The taste of passion was back in his kiss. This time, nothing would stop them. The scent of his presence filled her nostrils and she strove to hold herself just a little apart from his passion. She wanted to remember it all, every moment of these next days.

Maxim sensed her withdrawal, though she hadn't actually moved. "Are you cold?"

She opened her eyes. "I was trying to put into words your taste."

"My what?"

"You taste like spiced cider; warm and sweet and yet pungent."

Maxim shook his head. "I thought it was you."

"Maybe it's *us*," she suggested.

"Must be," he agreed a scant second before he blended their tastes once more.

"Georgie," he murmured after a moment, "Georgie, this stick shift is cutting into my thigh so badly I think the blood's stopped running in my leg. Let's go inside."

She sat up. "Go in?"

The vista before her took her breath away. She'd been prepared for the forest and the blue-green beauty of the mountains, but she had no words to express the beauty before her now.

They were on the edge of a silver-white river which curled in and then away from them. Beyond, great evergreens marched up the slope of a hill, their limbs edged in new-fallen snow. Farther up, where the trees blended into a solid mass of green, the snow seemed to be gathered in tiers like ermine tails on a vast emerald robe.

Her eyes found and followed a narrow path, a mere indentation in the snow, leading to the dark outline of a stone building. "It's a farm house!" she said in surprise.

"I told you not everything I owned was grand," Maxim replied. "You're not disappointed, are you?"

Surprised by his anxious tone, she turned to him. "I'd stay in a tree if you were there. But this," she said, gazing at the Pre–Revolutionary War building, "this is absolutely perfect!"

A grin lit up his face. "Come on, then. I've got a lot of work to do before we're set for the night."

The first thing she noticed was the huge fireplace that commanded half of one main wall. The second thing was that although the furnishings were good quality, they were definitely rustic. Heavy mahogany formed the frames of a sofa and chairs covered in quilted fabric. The effect was homey and warm. It was a place to relax and enjoy oneself.

"Okay?"

Her husky laughter filled the room to its rafters. "I love it, Maxim!"

"Come see the bedroom," he suggested with a devilish grin.

"I'm afraid the amenities have been held to a minimum here," he began, as he placed their bags on the bedroom floor. "There's a little electricity in the kitchen and one light in the main room. The plumbing's loud but functional. There's no phone or TV. No light in here but candles or oil lamp." While speaking he lit a table oil-lamp and replaced the globe.

With lamplight Georgianna discovered that a large Jacobean canopy bed with crocheted hangings and spread held sway in the small room. Pegged floors were covered by hand-knotted rugs. Next to the bed was another fireplace, with a hurricane chamber stick at each end.

"We'll eat and make love by candlelight," she said with quiet happiness.

"You really like it, don't you?"

She couldn't believe his concern. But it was there, in his face. "Why did you bring me here if you thought I might not like it?" she demanded with a grin.

He shrugged and placed his hands on his hips. "Because *I* like it."

It wasn't the only spontaneous laughter they shared that afternoon as they went about the business of building fires in both the bedroom and living room, and storing the supplies he had brought.

"I don't understand why I can't help," Georgianna complained an hour later as she sat wrapped in a blanket before the main fireplace.

"You slept a long time this afternoon," he called from the kitchen, "but that doesn't mean you're anywhere near well. The doctor wanted to keep you in the hospital. I sprung you. The least you can do is conserve what little strength you have so you can repay me properly when I've fed you."

"You think too much about food," she groused halfheartedly.

His head poked around the corner of the wall. "Did you take your medicine?"

"Yes." She waited until he disappeared before putting the painkiller in her pocket. It made her sleepy. If she took it, she wouldn't even know what was going on when they got into bed, and she had no intention of missing a second of it!

"You can cook when we marry," she suggested a little later when they sat side by side before the fire, the coffee table holding the remains of their meal.

"Why should I?" he asked, his arm tightening about her waist as he tucked a corner of her blanket securely in place.

"You'll be working on your book. You might as well make yourself useful," she reasoned.

"And what will you be doing?"

"Working. I do have some skills."

His hand slid up from her waist, the fingers spreading over her rib cage. "Show me."

Turning toward him was like turning her face to the sun, the most natural and easy thing she'd ever done. His lips found her mouth and parted, drawing her lips open, and his tongue made its way between them. Pleasure rippled through her.

"Georgie!" His voice was no more than a whispered breath against her mouth. "Georgie, I want you. I want to see you, touch you, feel myself deep inside you. Tell me that now is the moment."

"Yes!"

He didn't seem to react to her voice. His kisses merely continued skirting the outline of her mouth with maddening brevity until her mouth tingled with unfulfilled sensation.

"Please, please kiss me!" she murmured, stirring under the anchor of his arm which held her away from him and prevented her from deepening the pressure on his mouth.

"You've made me wait a long, long time, Georgie." He formed the words on her lips. "Don't be impatient. I want it all!"

Georgianna drew in a shuddering breath, hoping her all would be enough.

"You're cold?" he questioned.

"No. No, I'm not cold," she answered. He smiled and the sight calmed her. She raised her hand and cupped his chin, pulling it down to cover his mouth with her lips.

This time he held back nothing. Their kisses fed on one another, a feeling unlike any yet shared between them. Each touch, every nuance of pressure, every subtle scent heightened her awareness of the man in her arms.

When he parted the blanket about her, she leaned in against him. "Don't be shy," he encouraged, scooping a hand under the curve of her bottom to lift her toward him. "Better," he murmured as both hands grasped her bottom, the fingers sinking into the firm flesh to begin an erotic kneading. "You are all woman, Georgie. I've watched you walk, moving with such unconscious yet seductive grace. Do you know how beautiful you are?"

She shook her head. "No one's ever said that to me," she confessed.

Maxim stared into her eyes, hardly believing her words yet reading the truth in the golden-brown gaze regarding him. "Then you've known only fools, Georgie. You have the kind of quiet beauty that deserves to be cherished. I'll cherish you."

He bent to kiss her chin. "I cherish that stubborn jut of your chin. It caught my attention when you were still a stranger."

She chuckled in pure pleasure. "You're a flatterer, Maxim."

He stilled her laughter with a gentle, lingering kiss. "I cherish the husky quality in your voice, too. I feel like you've touched me deep inside whenever you say my name." He pulled her closer. "I thought I'd never hold you like this." He dipped his head, burrowing between the full mounds of her breasts.

Georgianna gasped and caught him about the neck as the moist heat of his breath penetrated her sweater and bra. Her hips moved under his hands as he molded her spine in an arch that pressed her tightly against him.

"I will love you always, Georgie, whatever happens!"

Released at last from any reluctance to enjoy being in his arms, she grew bold. She slipped through his arms into his lap. She glided a hand under the barrier of his sweater. Pressing with the heel of her palm, she slid her hand slowly up over the ridges of his ribs to the broad flat planes of his chest. With his help, she stripped it off him.

His body had fascinated her from the first. When he had stripped to chop wood for her, she had hardly been able to take her eyes away. Now she was free to look and feel and explore.

As his mouth descended on hers again, moist with heat and desire, her hand moved to the first button of his shirt. The buttons gave way, opening to her hand's inquisitive search. Her fingers spread inward over his hot skin, twining in the silky hairs. When she reached a nipple, its smoothness fascinated her and her finger rimmed it again and again, until he pulled back from her kiss to gasp deeply.

"Should I stop?" she whispered.

"Yes . . . next week," he answered hoarsely.

Bending her head, she replaced her hand with her lips, skimming lightly the contours of his chest. As her fingers swooped under his shirt to embrace his muscular back, she began to nibble at him softly.

He exhaled his breath in a shaky laugh. "If you're not careful, you're going to find yourself ravished right here on the floor!"

The power to so move him made her giddy. "You said I shouldn't be impatient," she reminded him, rising to nip his shoulder with her sharp teeth. "You said you wanted to enjoy it all."

"Maybe I should have said, Oh, Georgie! I don't think I can handle *all* right now!"

Before she could react, he caught her about the waist and flipped her back over his arm. Moving over her, he forced her onto her back. Without wasting a movement, he clasped her wrists in one hand and raised her arms above her head.

"Now," he said, the velvet-toned threat making her

stomach muscles contract in excitement. "Now it's my turn."

His other hand slipped under her sweater. When he found only the thin material of her bra his smile became wicked. "What was that you were doing? Ah, yes," he sighed as his finger found the soft crest of a breast. "Round and round, I go. Where I'll stop, only Georgie knows."

The words were silly, childish. Yet, there was nothing immature about her reaction to the erotic message his fingertip rubbed into the lush fullness of her breast. She closed her eyes, the better to feel the sensations and her own response. He was lying on her, his weight exciting in itself.

Abruptly, her mind came back to the motion of his hand as his fingers dipped into one lacy cup and closed on a breast. His other hand released her wrists and slipped under her, arching her upward. She felt the sudden loosening of her bra, and then the touch of cold air on her skin as he raised her up and peeled her clothing over her head.

Lying back, she opened her eyes to watch his reaction to her nakedness. As he gazed down at her the fire's reflected flames leaped in his eyes. "Lord, Georgie, you're more lovely than I imagined."

He cupped the fullness of one breast and bent his head to it. Pleasure streamed through her as his tongue touched the peak. Over and over, he lapped lightly at her, each stroke causing her to gasp softly. When he moved his head from one crest to the other, his tongue left a slick trail of delight in the valley between.

Georgianna moaned softly. A river of flame was running through her, beginning at her breasts, flowing rapidly down through her stomach, widening its path until it reached the apex of her thighs.

Before she could inure herself to the sweet torment, his approach changed and his teeth closed over one rigid peak. There was no pain but, oh, it was glorious agony as he sucked gently, tugging and stroking with his tongue.

"Please . . . plea— Oh, Maxim!"

She grasped his hair to pull his lips away, but he merely paused. "Trust me, Georgie. It's your pleasure. Enjoy it."

She couldn't think. And when she felt the zipper of her jeans slide open, she gave up trying. Moments later his hands were hot on her bare skin, the palms branding her with their possession.

She didn't realize that he, too, was now naked, until his knee parted hers and the muscled shape of his thigh invaded the space between.

Maxim rose up to look at her in the firelight. Her body was warm honey tones and taupe shadows and her hair caught the reflection of red-gold flames as it spread out on the blanket. Her eyes were wide with her new knowledge of him.

He smiled at her, happier than he could ever remember being. "I can cherish you best with my body."

Georgianna knew no cold while the river of desire he had unleashed ran in rapids through her body. His strong body molded itself into the softer impression of hers.

Moving eager and hard, their hips strained toward the

joining yet to come as their mouths blended in perfect union.

"Georgie, love . . . I can't . . . wait," he groaned finally.

He raised himself up, kneeling for a moment between her thighs to catch his breath. And then his hands were on her hips, lifting her slightly. He entered her in one swift movement, propelled through the barrier before he could fully record it. A cry of surprise came from her.

"Georgie?" Maxim whispered in stunned amazement.

She shook her head, refusing to open her eyes. He was sliding deeper into her, the feeling indescribable and irrefutable. This was the moment she had been waiting for, and it was worth it.

Maxim grasped her tightly in his arms, trying to ease her tension, but he couldn't remain completely still. The subtle rotation of his hips continued, a primitive and powerful force.

"I love you, Georgie," he whispered tenderly. "Feel me, feel me love you."

Slowly Georgianna's body absorbed the new sensations, registering each of his movements as a shock wave of ecstasy. She was part of him and he part of her.

*This is how it was meant to be,* she thought.

And then she stopped thinking at all.

Maxim knew the moment she was once more with him. She arched under him, seeking the sensation he wanted so badly to give her. He thrust slowly at first, every move carrying him deeper, until he felt himself drowning in her body. He groaned his relief when he heard her faint cries of "Yes, yes!" as her hands flexed on his back and his tempo changed quickly.

"Georgie! Georgie! I . . . love . . . you . . . so!"

Still coupled, needing to be as close as possible, they fell asleep on the floor. Both were filled with the pleasure they had created together.

# Chapter Thirteen

*M* axim bent, stirred the embers of the dying fire, and tossed another log into the bedroom fireplace. The room was so cold he could see his breath forming before his face when he moved to the window to look out. It was 3 A.M. In another few hours they would be on their way back to Plowden.

It was their third night together, and yet the thought of their first lovemaking would not leave his mind. It came back every time he touched her.

*He was Georgianna's first lover.*

The frigid air felt good against his naked body; it kept his mind off the dilemma before him. As long as he lay in bed beside her he couldn't think of anything else other than making love to her.

He smiled. Georgianna was so happy, so proud of his

love, and so eager to explore the world of sensual sensation they created together. He couldn't help wondering if any other woman had ever been as pleased with his lovemaking. He knew the answer. No one could have been because he had never before felt as passionate as he did in Georgianna's arms. She gave an extra dimension to his virility. With her it was not just sex; it was much more. She made him whole, finished the ragged edge of his life that had made him restless for so long. In three short days she'd become as necessary to him as breathing.

And now he was about to let her go, without the slightest idea of when he would see her again.

"Maxim?"

Georgianna was sitting up in bed, her shoulders bare above the covers. The sight not only aroused him, it annoyed him. "Go back to sleep, Georgie."

"Aren't you tired?"

"I'm bone-weary. Now go back to sleep. I won't attack you for at least another hour."

Georgianna pulled the covers up over her shoulders in a defensive gesture. Maxim was angry. He turned away, and the firelight illuminated his long body: the wide shoulders, the valley of his spine, the compact globes of his buttocks, the corded muscles of his thighs and calves. She knew each and every part of him; and right now she even knew what he was thinking. She could tell by the slight unfamiliar stoop of his shoulders that he wasn't happy.

She knew the cause of his unhappiness. It was the same thing that was keeping her awake. Later this very day they would part, and she had no better idea than he of when they could be together again.

"You're going to freeze," she ventured in a quiet voice.

She watched his head rise and his shoulders straighten.

"I'm not allowed to question you, Georgianna, but I demand the right to my own thoughts."

The rebuff in his voice struck her like an icy blast of wind, but she did not try to shield herself from it. Instead her heart ached for him. He was only human. She couldn't blame him for the thoughts chasing around in his head. And yet, never once during the entire weekend had he asked her a single forbidden question. She doubted she could have been as stoic. If only she could offer him something, some hope to ease his frustration.

"I'm not married, Maxim. I never have been."

He swung around, every line of his body rigid with surprise.

She hadn't meant to say that. But, once the words were out, she couldn't take them back. "I want to tell you everything, Maxim, but I can't! Please, please trust me a little longer!"

She paused, waiting in anxious fear for him to speak. He came and sat at the foot of the bed, just out of reach. "Who's Alan?"

Georgianna shook her head. "You promised me, no questions."

She heard him curse under his breath.

"I love you with all my heart. Please come to bed," she begged in a faint voice.

A shiver ran over Maxim's skin. Georgianna was not married. But she was hiding things from him, things she must fear his knowing . . . or things she feared his being a part of. "You're in some kind of trouble, aren't you?"

She lowered her head, unable to lie to him anymore. In another moment he would have the story out of her.

"I'm no fool, Georgianna. I know you're in some sort of danger. Is this man Alan protecting you? I hope to God he knows what he's doing!" he added when she did not respond.

"Tell me if there is anything I can do to help you."

Georgianna raised her head. "Hold me, hold me until the sun rises!"

He reached across the small space between them and embraced her. "Georgie, I can help. I know people, I have contacts. If someone is after you, if you've done something wrong and are hiding, I can help you."

Georgianna touched her cheek to his. "I haven't committed any crime, Maxim. I need only a little more time. I haven't been fair to you or—anyone."

Maxim's hold tightened until he knew he hurt her, but he couldn't let go. "I saw a stranger on the beach one day last September and I fell in love. When I found you again, you were no longer a dream—but you were just as unattainable. I wanted to strangle you when I learned you were married because, somehow, you'd become a part of me before I ever knew your name.

"Now you're asking me to let you go. I don't know if I can, Georgie."

He shook her lightly, as though he were trying to shake good sense into her. "You're dangerous, lady.

You're like a drug that I can't get enough of. Each time I say just one more taste, I find the longing for you returning like an unquenchable thirst. Tell me what I must do to ease the pain, Georgie. Tell me!''

Georgianna answered him in the only way she knew how, with her kisses and her body.

The cold weather had passed during the weekend. By the time they reached Danbury, the snow had all but melted from the surrounding countryside. But the warmth had brought the gray mist of rain and fog with it. The sky was leaden, the streets slick.

Looking out at the forbidding late afternoon gloom, both passengers in the Lamborghini felt that the day matched their moods perfectly.

When Maxim turned into the garage parking lot, Georgianna almost sighed aloud in relief. Neither of them had spoken a word during the last hour. Maxim's resentment of her secrecy had made him sullen to the point of rudeness, and she had not known how to reassure him without bringing up the problem between them.

Now, neither of them wanted this good-bye.

Georgianna reached for the door handle, her face averted from his. ''I'll call you,'' she said softly, and opened the door.

Maxim stopped her with a hand placed caressingly on the back of her neck. ''I love you, Georgianna.''

Georgianna bit her lip, willing herself to leave him but unable even to speak.

''It's been worth it,'' he continued quietly, lightly stroking his thumb up and down the silky surface of her nape. "We've had our wedding night. I mean to have our wedding . . . soon."

Her eyes were wide with anguish when she turned to him. "I'm sorry, Maxim. I never meant—I didn't know—!"

"Georgie, Georgie! Don't cry. Oh, baby, I'm the one who's sorry." He turned her face into his shoulder and held her tight. "I've been behaving like a spoiled brat, sulking because I can't have everything my way."

Georgianna clung to him. "I didn't know it would hurt this much to say good-bye," she whispered.

"But it's not good-bye." He pushed her back from him. "Georgie, look at me." When her wide dark eyes met his deep blue gaze, he smiled. "It's not good-bye, Georgie. It's only a brief parting."

"I hate it!" she answered fervently.

"Then call me, tonight. No, listen! I gave Barnes the weekend off. He has family in Boston. It was a holiday weekend and I certainly didn't need him. No one will answer my phone tonight but me." His expression softened. "And I'd like to know that you arrived home safe. Promise you'll do that much. Call me. Please."

With a surge of desperate longing, she realized she seldom heard Maxim say please. Without being told, she knew that he seldom begged anything of anyone.

"I'll call. I promise."

He let her go with a brief hard kiss. They couldn't have parted, and she knew it, if there had been anything more.

But Georgianna couldn't shake the anxiety of leaving him. Once on the highway, headed back to Plowden, she began to worry. Because there was no phone at Maxim's, she hadn't called Alan even once during the weekend. He would be furious with her. How would she explain to him that she'd just spent the weekend with a man? She wouldn't be surprised if he came to Plowden to get her.

*"You never stop to think, Georgianna. You act out of your emotions. When will you learn?"*

Georgianna cringed as her father's words came back to her. How often had he repeated them during her teen years?

"But I haven't done wrong, not really," she protested aloud.

She had fallen in love. That wasn't a crime. She couldn't go on allowing Maxim to believe that she was married, not after he knew that she'd never made love to any other man. Yet, she hadn't revealed her situation. And more important, she hadn't involved Maxim in any danger.

Yes, she decided, she must hold on to that thought as Alan barraged her with questions and accusations. She had kept Maxim safe. That was the most important thing of all.

But the anxiety didn't leave her. As she turned her car into Quaker Lane, her wounded arm ached from the tension of her hands gripping the steering wheel. She'd left the Rhoadses' house vacant for three days. As far as she knew, the man looking for her had not been apprehended.

As the house came into view, she knew a moment of pure panic. What if he had found her, had broken into the house, and now waited inside?

Georgianna exhaled and inhaled, trying to stabilize her pulse rate as she swung the car into the Rhoadses' driveway. There were lights on inside. That didn't surprise her. She'd set timers to correspond to her usual routine. It was nearly dark, time for her to be moving in and out of the kitchen and living room.

She didn't give herself time to lose courage by sitting in the car. She swung open the door and hopped out the moment the engine died. As soon as she got inside she would call Maxim. That thought gave her courage. It would be worth braving the silent house to hear his voice.

The key went easily into the lock and turned. The door swung open into a lighted but empty hallway and Georgianna blew out a loud breath which ended in shaky laughter.

"Georgianna, you coward!" she said in mocking tones, shoving the door shut. There was nothing to fear but her own guilt at having left. Maxim! She would call Maxim.

She'd taken no more than three steps into the hallway when a silhouette appeared on the landing of the hall stairway. She froze, the blood in her veins suddenly ice water as she watched the form of a man appear.

"Where the hell have you been!"

That voice!

"A–Alan?" she stuttered as he descended the stairs.

"Did I frighten you?" the stranger asked. "Good! You deserve worse."

"Alan?" she repeated less anxiously.

He nodded once.

Even before that, relief had begun unknotting the fear in the pit of her stomach. This was not the man she feared, though his face was very angry.

His hair was golden blond; a thick shock of it fell over his brow, drawing her gaze to his hazel eyes. His chin was square and he was smooth-shaven in spite of his sleepy appearance. He was in his shirtsleeves, his suit pants wrinkled as though he had slept in them. Suddenly Georgianna knew why he was familiar.

"You posed for the picture of Edward!" she cried, indignant and incredulous at the idea.

For the first time he smiled. "It's an old photo. I graduated from Annapolis ten years ago. Served four years aboard a submarine. That's what gave me the idea for your cover in the first place." His gaze moved approvingly over her. "You're prettier than your pictures."

Georgianna knew a moment of pure rage. "How dare you stand there so calmly! You nearly frightened me to death!"

Not answering, he moved quickly past her, picked up the phone in the kitchen hall, and dialed. "She's home," he barked into the receiver, and then hung up.

His smile disappeared as he came back to stand before her in the front hall. "Let me tell you something, lady, you're not feeling half of what I felt when I realized you weren't here on Thursday.

"That's right. I left my wife and kids and twenty pounds of turkey to drive down here from Hartford. I had to pick the Rhoadses' lock and then knock on your neighbors' doors until I found one who recalled seeing you drive away earlier in the day. An all-points bulletin didn't locate your car until noon on Friday. By then I had four agents in the field looking for you. It took Aunt Cora to put us on the right path.''

*"Aunt Cora?"* Georgianna echoed.

The front door opened and Georgianna wasn't surprised to see Cora's silver head appear. "Georgianna! My dear!''

The older woman hurried up to throw her arms about Georgianna. "I blame myself," she continued, sniffing back what would have been tears. "In all my experience I've never lost a witness. And then this!'' Her gray eyes were bright with emotion. "You should have confided in me, Georgianna. Didn't you think I knew how you felt about your young man?''

Georgianna shook her head, trying to clear the whirlwind of confusion spinning about in there. "I don't understand any of this. You, Cora, were a part of—of spying on me?''

Cora clucked her tongue in disapproval. "You must never think of it as that. Alan, dear, take Georgianna's coat. She must be exhausted. Then come into the living room, both of you. We must sort this all out.''

Georgianna allowed herself to be maneuvered into the room and onto the sofa before bursting out with, "I can't believe this! You, Cora, were watching me all the time?''

Her gaze switched to Alan. "Why did you lie to me, letting me think I was on my own?''

Alan leaned back in a chair and folded his arms across his chest. "The orders came from higher up. My boss said you were pretty shook up by what had happened to you. Then that client of yours turned up murdered—''

"Murdered?" Georgianna repeated in horror.

Alan's gaze met Cora's. "Tell her. I knew you should have," Cora prompted.

"Estacio Gonzales was working for the men you saw commit murder. We have reason to believe that the boy was deliberately given an overdose of drugs. We don't know why, and it doesn't really matter. But it was definitely murder. The men you're pointing a finger at have big connections. We didn't want you to be any more frightened than necessary."

Georgianna's vision was blurred by tears, but her voice was firm. "You were afraid that if I knew about Estacio I would change my mind—out of fear—and refuse to testify." She shook her head in amazement. "None of you know me very well. What you've told me only makes me more determined to see justice done. Estacio wasn't what you'd call a good kid, but he deserved better; any child does. And he was, after all, a child."

Cora nodded in approval. "Now, I should explain my part. I'm not an agent, Georgianna. I really am a retired schoolteacher with a passion for violets and minding other people's business." A cherubic smile curved her mouth. "But I have occasionally worked with Alan's bosses over the years. You never asked me about my husband, what sort of work he was in. I know it was because you didn't want me to feel free to question you in turn. But it worked to my advantage, too. My Daniel was a federal agent. It was his idea for us to work for the

Justice Department after he retired early. We lived in a small town, were respectable citizens. We were perfect chaperons for federal witnesses needing temporary shelter. Don't look shocked. There are many of us throughout the country. It's because you'd never suspect us of anything secretive that we're useful. Who do you think recommended you for this house-sitting job?''

She gave Georgianna's hand a sympathetic pat. ''When Alan phoned, asking me if I could help out, everything seemed to fall into place. You wanted independence and I needed an excuse to keep an eye on you. House-sitting for the neighbors was ideal.''

Georgianna tried to digest this piece of information, but it only succeeded in making her angry. ''You must have found me foolish, mooning around, pretending to be in love, when all the time you knew it was a sham.''

''Quite the contrary, dear. I applauded your performance. You were perfect, holding me off when I badgered you with questions. And when Maxim De Hoop came on the scene, well, I held my breath. I wasn't aware that you'd gone ahead with your pretense, letting him believe you were married, until he called me one day with a cock-and-bull story about wanting to invite you and your husband to dinner.'' She chuckled. ''Poor dear, how he's suffered. Believe me, when he told me that he loved you, I couldn't pretend any longer.''

''He told you that he loves me? When?''

Cora beamed at her. ''I knew he'd told me before he'd confessed it to you. He told me the night you injured yourself.''

''About that,'' Alan cut in. ''What happened?''

"I confused the backfire of a motorcycle with gunfire," Georgianna said in a low voice as she touched the bandage Maxim had changed earlier in the day.

"I told Alan it had nothing to do with an attempt on you," Cora said. "I'd never have gone into Manhattan had I thought otherwise."

"But you acted like you didn't know Alan when he called," Georgianna protested.

It was Alan's turn to smile. "Aunt Cora can be pretty impressive when need be. She kept her head throughout that crisis. But you frightened both of us when you disappeared Thursday."

Georgianna blushed. "If you haven't guessed, I was with Maxim De Hoop."

"We know, dear," Cora replied.

"When we'd traced your car to the parking lot, our man interviewed the owner," Alan explained. "He told us that De Hoop had made arrangements to meet a young woman at the garage, and they'd driven off together and weren't expected back until today." Alan's knowing look brought a blush to her face. "Once we knew you were safe, I decided to wait here."

Georgianna couldn't quite meet their eyes. It was embarrassing to know that strangers were aware of her personal business. Then she thought about Maxim and she raised her head. "We're going to be married, when this is all over."

"Wonderful!" Cora exclaimed.

"So you told him," Alan replied more reservedly.

"I did not!" Georgianna maintained. "I merely told him I wasn't really married and that he must trust me."

Alan snorted. "And he agreed? Well, one never knows what a man will do for love. But that doesn't solve our immediate problem, which is to get you out of here, pronto!"

"Why?" Georgianna looked at first one and then the other of them. "If you're worried about Maxim interfering, he promised not to even try to see me until I call him. And I don't plan to do that until the trial date is set." Her eyes widened in hope. "Is that it, has the date been decided upon?"

"Haven't you wondered why I'd waste a whole weekend here, waiting for you to come back from your—ah, holiday?"

"Something's happened." Georgianna's scalp tingled. "You've located the man out on bail?"

Alan reached for the newspaper on the table in front of him and flipped it open. "It's the *New York Times*, Friday morning edition."

Georgianna leaned forward, dreading the moment her eyes would focus. What was it, what could be so horrible that Alan's voice had become so cool and formal? Hand trembling slightly, she reached for the paper.

It was opened to a page of photographs. The headline read, "New England Autumn: The Season For Dreamers." The first pictures were of common sights caught with refreshing clarity: fallen leaves, a bonfire. Others were less ordinary. Her eyes paused a moment on the pair of aged intertwined hands. A couple in the autumn of their lives; Georgianna smiled at this interpretation of the title. It sounded like something Maxim—

She glanced at the photo credit. "These are Maxim's pictures!"

"Yes." Alan bit out the word. "Now look at the final shot."

"Oh, no!" It was a close-up of her face. And while it was only a three-quarters profile, it caught her likeness with an uncanny reality. Even the scar on her cheek was visible.

"You saw this, that's what kept you here," she said softly.

"Me and half the country," Alan answered sourly. "Your boyfriend sold this spread to a national news service. It appeared all over the country on Friday. When you didn't answer your phone I knew my a—rear was on the line. Why the hell did you let him do this!"

"I didn't," Georgianna whispered, running her finger over the picture. Maxim had promised her a nice surprise when she returned. Little did he know how awful it was in reality. "I didn't know he had taken these pictures, believe me."

"Well, it's too late now. You're back, safe, and that's all that matters. We're transferring you out of the state. I've put in a call to the man who'll meet you in New York tonight. I've booked you a flight out of Kennedy. Don't ask to tell you where you're going. I've got to insist on secrecy at the moment."

Georgianna wasn't listening. Something was circling in her mind, something that she couldn't quite put her finger on. Just because her picture had appeared in the paper, that didn't mean anyone would know exactly where to find her. The setting of New England covered a lot of territory. She would still be difficult to locate. But . . . they . . . could . . . locate—

"Maxim!"

Georgianna shot to her feet. "They'll be looking for Maxim! The photo credit is his. They'll try to make him tell them where I am. Oh, Alan, we've got to warn him!"

Alan beat her to the phone. "Give me the guy's number. I'll tell him what he needs to know."

Georgianna repeated it, her voice quaking. She had wanted to shield Maxim, to protect him from danger. Now, because of her, he was right in the middle of it without any knowledge or warning.

"There's no answer," Alan said grimly.

"He's home! He said he'd be. He made me promise to call!" Georgianna replied. Her throat muscles contracted with fear until she could hardly breathe.

*Oh, dear God, please let him be all right!*

Alan hung up and dialed the operator. "Check this number. It's an emergency. I've got to get through," he rapped out. "You say the phone's out of order?"

With a muffled curse he hung up and began dialing a new number. Over his shoulder he said, "Aunt Cora, go upstairs and get my coat and keys. I'm calling the police."

With Alan absorbed in his conversation, Georgianna began backing away, slowly at first. When she heard Cora's rapid steps on the stairs, she turned and ran. Her purse was on the living-room table. She didn't even look for her coat. Maxim was in trouble. That was the cause of the premonition that had hounded her all the way from

Danbury. If he was hurt or in danger, it was her fault. She had to get there and help him!

She took the front steps two at a time, the mist of rain on her cheeks barely registering as she struggled to get the key from the depths of her purse.

"Damn it!" she cried, ripping the lining as the key came free. At first she couldn't find the lock and then the key seemed to be the wrong one. Finally, left-handed, she slid it into place and turned it, popping up the lock.

As she swung the door open, hands grabbed her from behind and turned her around.

"What the hell do you think you're doing now?"

Georgianna struggled in his grip. "Please! I've got to go to him! He knows nothing! He won't be expecting trouble!"

For what seemed an eternity, Alan held her tight. "All right!" he said, relenting. "But I'm driving, and you're staying in the car until the police arrive. Understood?"

She didn't even answer. She dropped the keys in his hand and then climbed in the driver's side and slid over to make room for him. "Hurry!"

Alan handled the car with ease, but it seemed to Georgianna that he drove at a snail's pace. "Please hurry. He should have been home for nearly half an hour. He's alone. There's no one there to help him. Hurry!"

Alan glanced at her. "If I'd known you were going to go and fall in love on me, I'd have locked you up." His humor did not get a reaction. "Look," he said more sympathetically. "De Hoop could have been in the john when I called."

"Nice try. The phone's out of order," Georgianna reminded him through gritted teeth.

Alan brushed her cheek with a hand and found it wet. "If the worst is true, that they've located De Hoop, there's no reason to assume that they'd hurt him. After all, they want your address. They might be quite pleasant about the whole matter."

She didn't bother to contradict him. Maxim was no fool. He'd guessed that she was in trouble. If someone came looking for her, especially if they knew her by another name, he would put two and two together and try to protect her. If he did that, there was no telling what might happen.

She squeezed her eyes shut. She'd been crying without making a sound. Now, suddenly, the tears stopped. She felt cold inside, colder and more afraid than she had ever been. But the cold made her calm, the frigid kind of calm that sometimes comes when one is waiting for tragic news.

She didn't even stop to wonder how Alan knew the way to Maxim's home. Even when he slowed up to look for the hidden drive, she didn't think to offer any aid. She was deep in thought, remembering Maxim's handsome face crinkled with laughter, his eyes heavy with passion, his face tense on the brink of fulfillment. It wasn't possible to believe that she would never see him like that again. He just must, must be all right! Silent prayers formed in her mind.

*Please! Please, God! Let Maxim be all right! We've just found one another! Please don't let anything hurt him! Not because of me! I love him, love him so!*

The house came into view, but there were no cars in the drive. The police had yet to arrive.

"Dammit!" Alan muttered as he eased the car into the circle before the front door. "You stay put!" he ordered without even glancing at Georgianna.

Georgianna didn't wait for his door to close before she bolted out and ran toward the house. She heard Alan's cry die in mid-shout as he remembered that it might alert the wrong person. He caught up with her at the door.

"Will you go back!" he hissed.

Frantic, she jerked away from him, stumbled, and fell heavily against the door. The door gave way under her weight, swinging wide and sending her sprawling to the floor. Groping wildly, she tried to catch herself with her left hand as the door crashed back against the wall.

There was a shout from the direction of the living room, and then everything seemed to happen at once.

The sound of a shot was followed by a man's cry and scuffling noises. Alan bolted past her, drawing a pistol from his coat pocket. Out on the drive tires skidded as a police siren whined to life.

From far away she heard Alan cry "Halt!" and then there were two more shots.

Georgianna struggled to rise, holding her bandaged hand close to her body because she'd fallen on it. Suddenly there were helping hands as two policemen came up behind her and lifted her to her feet.

"Please! In there! Help them!" she begged, pointing to the living room. One of the policemen moved forward as the other held her firmly by the arm.

"We need an ambulance!"

Her heart contracted painfully at the sound of Alan's voice. More police hurried through the door.

"Let me go!" she demanded of the policeman holding her. "I've got to know if it's . . . it's . . ." She couldn't say it. The thought was too terrible.

Suddenly Alan was before her, his face grim. "It's over. De Hoop's going to be okay, but he's been hurt, Georgianna."

With a whimper of pain she broke from the policeman's grasp and ran into the living room.

She hardly recognized the beautiful room she had seen only once before. Several of the tables were overturned and glass was scattered over the carpet. Her gaze swung wildly around the room, registering the still form of the man sprawled in one corner. Her heart stopped.

"Georgie?"

The sound of his voice—dear Lord, how good it sounded!—brought Georgianna back to reality. She turned toward one of the chairs flanking the double doors and saw Maxim sitting there. A policeman was stuffing cloth inside his left shirt front, but Maxim held out his right hand to her.

"Come here," he said softly.

She wasn't sure her legs would support her and she doubted they would have if it hadn't been for his eyes on her. Her feet hardly seemed to touch the floor as she covered the distance between them. He was covered in blood on the left side, but he was smiling at her, as if he had only awakened to find her in his bed.

"Oh, Maxim! I'm so sorry!" she cried, kneeling down and throwing her arms about him.

"It's going to be okay, Georgie girl," he said softly, hugging her to his good side. "It's going to be just fine."

Georgianna had never been fond of hospitals, but nothing could have dragged her away from the emergency waiting room. For what seemed like days she sat with Cora, too numb to try to make conversation. Maxim had received a bullet high in the fleshy part of his left shoulder. If the aim had been better or his movement wrong, he could have—

A trembling began within her. She couldn't believe how calm she had been once her first tears were over. She had waited patiently for the ambulance, holding onto Maxim's hand like it was the lifeline to her own existence.

She had ridden in the back with him, talking softly and calmly while he lay quietly watching her. She couldn't explain what had happened to him and why, not then. She had talked about her drive back from Danbury, about her love for the countryside of New England, about anything but the reality of the moment.

"Miss Helton?"

Georgianna looked up into the face of the emergency-room doctor to see him smiling down at her. "Mister De Hoop is about to be taken upstairs. Once he's in his room, you may visit him. He's been asking for you since he arrived. Room three seventeen."

"Thank you," she said, clasping his hand. "You're certain he's going to be all right?"

"Right as rain. He's a tough man. He was telling me

about the first time someone shot at him while I worked on him. He's got nerves of steel.''

Georgianna shook her head. She didn't want to know about anyone shooting at the man she loved. His profession would have to change somewhat when they married.

*Married!*

Georgianna sank back down in her seat. ''Oh, Cora, what can I say to him?''

Cora took the younger woman's hands in hers. ''Tell him the truth. You may be surprised. I would suspect that he's guessed a great part of it. The police will have talked with him, certainly.''

''But, Cora, he was almost killed because of me!''

Cora gave her a sharp, no-nonsense glare. ''That young man nearly got *himself* killed! If he had asked your permission to use your photograph, this could have been prevented. Don't you feel guilty over what happened. You did everything you could to keep him out of danger.''

Georgianna let out a shaky breath. ''If I'd discouraged him more. . . .''

Cora's brows rose. ''Discouraged him? I don't recall you chasing him. He did the chasing, my dear, and he thought *you* were married. He's been at fault on more than one score. But, of course, that's all behind us now.''

Georgianna couldn't help but smile. ''You're a nice person, Cora, and a good friend.''

Cora's cheeks reddened. ''You're not angry over my little deception? You were absolutely furious with Alan.''

Georgianna shook her head. ''I was only angry in the beginning. Thank goodness he was there tonight.''

''Do I hear my praises being sung?'' Alan had walked out of the Emergency Room and was smiling down at her. ''I should be furious with you. You could have gotten yourself killed. How would that have looked on my record?''

Georgianna stood and put her arms around Alan. ''Thank you for saving Maxim's life.''

''That fiancé of yours is something else. He was absolutely calm as he told me about his unexpected visitor. De Hoop wouldn't admit knowing you, of course, and that was the cause of the trouble. They were discussing the issue over the barrel of a gun when we arrived. Your instincts were right. I just thank the saints I got a clear shot.''

''The man's dead?'' Georgianna asked the question even though she knew the answer.

Alan nodded. ''So, all that's left is for the man who's still in jail to stand trial. I don't think his buddies will continue to back a lame horse. He'll find himself on his own after this incident. I don't look for any more trouble.''

Alan hugged her briefly. ''Now go on upstairs and see your man. Take your time. I'll still be here when you come down.''

Georgianna began a dozen explanations on the elevator. Nothing sounded right. How could she apologize for what had happened? He might have been killed. She should have warned him, given him a chance to be prepared. But she hadn't because she'd thought that he was safer knowing nothing.

She stood staring at his door for a full minute. She couldn't make the words come out right. She pushed the door open.

He was lying almost flat on the bed, his face inordinately pale beneath the natural tan of his skin. But his eyes sparkled when he recognized her. "Hi, Georgie."

She'd never thought of herself as a crier, but she hadn't been able to turn off the tears in the last few hours. They flooded her vision now, blurring his image. "Oh, Maxim, I'm so—"

"So, so, sorry," he finished for her in gentle laughter.

Georgianna started at the sound, her back stiffening in offense. "You . . . you may think it's funny . . . b—but it's . . . it's not," she said over the funny catch in her voice.

"Georgie, come here," he directed gently, holding out a hand to her. "Come on," he coaxed as she stood rigidly by the door. "Or don't you think I've done enough chasing in this relationship?"

"You mean you expect me to do the chasing from now on?" she ventured in a stronger voice as she moved slowly toward the bed.

He grinned at her and a little of his color returned. "It seems to me that we should both stand still. It's so much easier to make love that way." Maxim's hand closed over hers, warm and firm and, wonderfully, his.

"I never meant this to happen," she said softly, drinking in his features as if it had been months instead of hours since they'd seen one another. "I didn't want you placed in danger because of me. Yet, just look what's happened to you."

"What happened was my own fault. I knew I was taking a chance when I sold your photo without obtaining your permission. I wanted to surprise you. I thought the worst that could happen would be that I'd be sued, not shot."

"Don't joke about it, it's too awful."

He tugged on her arm. "I need you a little closer, Georgie. I'm cold."

With a little cry of relief, Georgianna bent over him, covering his face with wild sweet kisses. She didn't even protest as he urged her into his bed and then pulled her down alongside him.

"There, that's much better," he said as she nestled against him, the tears released yet again. "You're turning into a regular waterworks, Georgie girl," he protested gently. "Is that how you plead your cases in court, with a suggestive wiggle of your lovely behind and a few tears?"

She raised her head from his shoulder to gaze down at him. "You know about that, too?"

He nodded. "I know everything. Well, almost. I know that you're a lawyer in Maryland and what you've been doing here in Plowden. Alan told me everything, a kind of trade of information. I even know about Cora's part in all this."

"And you forgive me for all my deceptions?" she whispered, her eyes lowering before his.

He drew her chin up with a crooked finger. "Remember when I told you that not everybody can change the world, but that there are those who do what they can and that their contributions are what make the world go round? You're one of those precious people, Georgie. I knew you were special from the moment I first saw you.''

Georgianna nodded, loving him more than she thought possible. "You do understand."

"I do."

She smiled through her tears. "Then I don't see what you could possibly not know."

"Our wedding date, Georgie girl. Our wedding date."

She traced the shape of his brow with her fingertips. "I've always thought December weddings were kind of nice. Of course, I don't want to live in that museum you call a house." Stricken by what she'd said, she bit her lip. "Oh, Maxim, the living room was badly damaged. Things were broken, tables overturned."

Laughter rumbled in his chest before it reached his lips. "Barnes will have apoplexy," he agreed, and guffawed.

"Oh, Georgie, I know it's a shame to say so, but I've never liked that room. The loss of a few antiques won't hurt us. We'll redecorate."

She shook her head. "I don't want my children raised in that stuffy atmosphere."

"Your children?" he repeated, passion glimmering in his eyes. "Our children," he corrected. "And, if you're very, very good, I may just have a surprise for you when I get out of here."

"Let's live in the Vermont farmhouse," she suggested.

He shook his head. "Too cold. But there's somewhere I've been wanting to take you since the day I first saw you."

"It must have a bed in it," Georgianna ventured smugly.

A smile of pure lust lit up Maxim's features as he pictured Georgianna sprawled deliciously naked beneath him in great-grandfather Willem De Hoop's schooner bed.

"As a matter of fact, it does!"

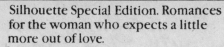

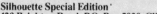

# Silhouette Special Edition

## MORE ROMANCE FOR
## A SPECIAL WAY TO RELAX

### $2.25 each

# Silhouette Special Edition

## $2.25 each

| | | | |
|---|---|---|---|
| 183 ☐ Sinclair | 189 ☐ Ripy | 195 ☐ Griffin | 201 ☐ Dalton |
| 184 ☐ Daniels | 190 ☐ Wisdom | 196 ☐ Cates | 202 ☐ Thornton |
| 185 ☐ Gordon | 191 ☐ Hardy | 197 ☐ Lind | 203 ☐ Parker |
| 186 ☐ Scott | 192 ☐ Taylor | 198 ☐ Bishop | 204 ☐ Eagle |
| 187 ☐ Stanford | 193 ☐ John | 199 ☐ Roberts | |
| 188 ☐ Lacey | 194 ☐ Jackson | 200 ☐ Milan | |

------------------------------------------------

**SILHOUETTE SPECIAL EDITION,** Department SE/2
1230 Avenue of the Americas
New York, NY 10020

Please send me the books I have checked above. I am enclosing $_____
(please add 75¢ to cover postage and handling. NYS and NYC residents please
add appropriate sales tax). Send check or money order—no cash or C.O.D.'s
please. Allow six weeks for delivery.

NAME _____

ADDRESS _____

CITY _____ STATE/ZIP _____

## Coming Next Month

### TIME AND TIDE
by Dixie Browning

•

### THE BITTER WITH THE SWEET
by Lucy Hamilton

•

### WIND SHADOW
by Renee Roszel

•

### PRIDE'S FOLLY
by Tracy Sinclair

•

### PROMISE HER TOMORROW
by Margaret Ripy

•

### A CORNER OF HEAVEN
by Sondra Stanford

# *Fall in love again for the first time every time you read a Silhouette Romance novel.*

## *Take 4 books free—no strings attached.*

Step into the world of Silhouette Romance, and experience love as thrilling as you always knew it could be. In each enchanting 192-page novel, you'll travel with lighthearted young heroines to lush, exotic lands where love and tender romance wait to carry you away.

**Get 6 books each month before they are available anywhere else!**
Act now and we'll send you four touching Silhouette Romance novels. They're our gift to introduce you to our convenient home subscription service. Every month, we'll send you six new Silhouette Romance books. Look them over for 15 days. If you keep them, pay just $11.70 for all six. Or return them at no charge.

We'll mail your books to you *two full months before they are available anywhere else.* Plus, with every shipment, you'll receive the Silhouette Books Newsletter absolutely free. *And Silhouette Romance is delivered free.*

Mail the coupon today to get your four free books—and more romance than you ever bargained for.

*...joy romance and passion, larger-than-life...*

# Now, thrill to 4 Silhouette Intimate Moments novels (a $9.00 value)— ABSOLUTELY FREE!

If you want more passionate sensual romance, then Silhouette Intimate Moments novels are for you!

In every 256-page book, you'll find romance that's electrifying...involving... and intense. And now, these larger-than-life romances can come into your home every month!

## 4 FREE books as your introduction.

Act now and we'll send you four thrilling Silhouette Intimate Moments novels. They're our gift to introduce you to our convenient home subscription service. Every month, we'll send you four new Silhouette Intimate Moments books. Look them over for 15 days. If you keep them, pay just $9.00 for all four. Or return them at no charge.

We'll mail your books to you *as soon as they are published.* Plus, with every shipment, you'll receive the Silhouette Books Newsletter absolutely free. *And Silhouette Intimate Moments is delivered free.*

Mail the coupon today and start receiving Silhouette Intimate Moments. Romance novels for women...not girls.

## *Silhouette Intimate Moments*

---